DANCE LIKE NO ONE IS WATCHING & OTHER STORIES

JAYA BALANTRAPU

Contents

Contents

Contents

Foreword

I am so happy that Jaya has finally published her first collection of short stories. We met on the beautiful island of Mauritius nearly 15 years ago. It was a place where the many moods of the Indian Ocean, the changing hues of the sky, and the peace and pace of island life inspired an abundance of literary ideas. It definitely inspired Jaya.

She has always had a literary bent of mind, and in our conversations, I noticed sparks of creativity and was sure this day, when she becomes a published author would come sooner rather than later. Those of you who have read her stories on social media will agree. I often told her to get her work published, and had even offered to help with the process. Sadly I couldn't keep my word, but I'm delighted to see that has not stopped her.

If you have just picked up this book, you are in for a treat. Memorable, believable characters take life on these pages, navigating relatable twists and turns of life. Whether it is an anxious daughter-in-law eager to please an exacting mother-in-law, or an audacious grandmother-granddaughter duo, or the familiarity of long-term relationships, you will find someone and something to relate to as you go through these bite-sized sketches with their vivid detail and natural dialogues.

My warmest best wishes to Jaya to keep delighting her readers and well wishers. I am certain her maiden endeavour will not be her only work, and I am sure you will share my belief when you have finished reading these stories.

Shantanu

A fellow book-lover and writer, friend and fan

(Shantanu Mukharji IPS(retired) & former National Security Advisor(NSA) to the Prime Minister of Mauritius.

Acknowledgements

I wholeheartedly thank the following.....................
My dear husband Venkat Balantrapu for painstakingly doing
all the work, including pushing me towards this accomplishment!
He has always been of support and encouraged me to try things
different than those I have been doing in my life. Thanks for
everything..!
My elder daughter Apoorva Balantrapu for designing the
beautiful book cover.
My younger daughter Akshara Balantrapu for the critical
inputs added by her .
My partners in crime, my hardest critics and greatest
supporters.
All my extended family and friends for their support and
appreciation which made this book happen.
I dedicate this book to my dear father, who is always there with
me..!

1

MOON WAKE

Rajesh was busy till late night doing his assignments to be submitted to his college final exams. A studious and intelligent student who always stood first in his class from his primary school, he was arrogant and always found his twin sister very annoying. His parents called her a dreamer, but he perceived her dumb and uninterested in her studies. Rajani was full of compassion and always volunteered to help others with her time and money.

Hey, what's up? Up so early? Done with your assignments? asked Rajesh sarcastically. No bhayya! But don't worry, I will do them tonight. Yesterday, I was with Chotu in the cancer ward as he had chemo and was in a very bad state. I was there to help him. Just sat there with him, reciting rhymes and stories. Hope he will be better today, poor chap" said Rajani, as if assuring herself.

Who are you? Mother Theresa and Dalai Lama rolled into one? Always at a hospital or some kennel or orphanage. Attending either to humans or animals! Why don't you mind your own business and study well? Dad and mom are spending thousands on our education and you just roam around, wasting your time and their money, yelled an irate Rajesh. His mom came hurriedly out of her room leaving her clients, to see what the commotion was all about.

Manjula quickly assessed the situation and said, "Rajesh, leave her alone. We never questioned your interest in only academics. Similarly, we respect Rajani's interest in varied fields. You don't worry about her wasting our money. We are perfectly fine with it. Now, stop all this yelling and go and do your work and let me do mine. I have few important clients in the office and next time, please keep your voice down," admonished Manjula before disappearing into her office room.

Rajesh's eyes were like daggers as he left fuming, cursing Rajani under his breath.

Dr.Rajesh, MBBS, MD, FRCS (London), the golden letters on the board proclaimed.

The huge multi-storied hospital building was brightly lit and centrally air-conditioned.

The medical personnel were walking briskly in and out of the rooms, but the atmosphere was of cool and calm efficiency. Dr.Rajesh came out of the operation theatre after finishing a gruelling surgery after a marathon 8 hours. The patient was responding well and Rajesh left with a smile of triumph on his face.

Saab, sab thayyaar(Sir, everything is ready), called Ramu. Yes, coming. Rajesh came out of his room and sat in the car. Dr.Jamuna, shouted say my "hi" to Rajani. Do ask her to come over for a dinner date along with Samir"."Sure dear", replied Rajesh, throwing a flying kiss and waving bye to his wife.

The car travelled swiftly for few hours and by evening, reached its destination.

The huge colourful garden and the cool breeze welcomed the weary travellers.

Rajani came out running, calling "bhayya"! Hope you had a comfortable journey.

"Yes, but now it's a monthly affair and I look forward to meeting you both in personal as well as professional capacity", said Rajesh with a smile.

Samir also joined them and they all walked into the spacious living room.

The dining table was arranged with all of Rajesh's favourite food and Anand was there, ready to serve the food to his favourite guest. Rajesh greeted Anand with a smile and sniffed hard, showing his appreciation. "Mutton biryani", he exclaimed to the delight of Anand who immediately launched into serving his guest of honour with utmost devotion.

Next morning, Rajesh, after his breakfast, went to meet Rajani in her posh clinic. His heart swelled with pride looking at her name on the door, Dr.Rajani MBBS, MD, Psychiatry. He still remembered how he treated her during their college days. When she failed in the entrance of medical examination, while he fared well, he ridiculed her and advised her to get married. He was merciless in his criticism. She took everything in her stride and tried again and succeeded in becoming a doctor. She never reacted to his discouragement and always maintained her dignity and never lost her vision. She proved that just being a nerd is not enough by becoming a very popular student in the medical college, liked by both students and professors alike. Finally, by bagging the best all-rounder student award, she proved her mettle. She was like a moon wake, spreading her light on the vast ocean.

His sister is now his therapist for his stress and anxiety which are a part of any successful surgeon's life. His busy schedule and the trauma of his patients and their relatives inevitably created lot of stress and he needed an outlet for that. Luckily, for him, his loving sister became an anchor, both on personal and professional fronts.

She treated him as a psychiatrist as well as a loving twin and that double dose was what kept him going well in life. She never showed any malice for the way he treated her when they were young. Instead, she behaved very affectionately and efficiently and pulled him out of his dark phase. She and husband Samir complement each other in their compassion and love for social commitment.

His irritating and lazy sister whom he always looked down was now his life saver.

She was like a moon wake, a white light leading the ship of his life.

2

MATCH STICK

"Santakaram bhujaga sayanam", chanted Sharma, while taking out the agarbathi from the box and fixing it in the silver holder and then continued, "Padmanabham Suresham" while searching for the matchbox in the basket kept with all other puja items on the shelf. "Viswadharam! ....Shanta! Where is the match box? shouted Sharma.

Will be there in the basket. Check properly, shouted back Shanta, making rotis in the kitchen. "Why will I ask if it is there? In this house, nothing is kept in its place", grumbled Sharma.

"Ya, it is my house. I only live here, isn't it? I am responsible for everything. What about you? Are you a guest or do you live in the next house?" retorted Shanta, angrily.

"Yesterday, after lightning the Diya, I told you that the matchbox had only one matchstick and asked you to refill the matchsticks from the jumbo box in the cupboard. Instead, you threw the box. Now, I can't even do it myself. What do you do the whole day, I don't understand?" exclaimed Sharma.

"I don't do anything. I have the Akshayapatra, like Draupadi to feed all of you.

Then a genie turns on the washing machine, irons your clothes, arranges the house and does the shopping for all our needs. I just chill and enjoy Netflix.

From morning 6.30, I am slogging here in the kitchen, making coffee, breakfast, packing lunch boxes, etc., and you can't even find a matchbox. Okay, I forgot about it. Agree. So what? You could have done it yourself, yesterday itself.

Finding the match box also comes under my duty, eh! You can only light the agarbathi". Shanta went on a war footing.

"Enough! No peace at home. I will go off to the Himalayas to find some", wailed Sharma. "Please do that. I am hearing that threat from the past decade. Just go away and let me have some peace", yelled back Shanta.

Sharma angrily went inside, got ready, took his laptop bag and left for his office.

"He finds something or other to spoil everyone's mood in the morning.

He has now left without his lunch box. He will eat something at the roadside and in the evening, we will have an early Diwali bomb blast" said Shanta, going out to check on him.

"Sorry, granny" said ten year old Krishna, who witnessed the whole scene from his room. Krishna was here on vacation to his Mamayya's house(maternal uncle).

Why? What did you do? enquired Lakshmi.

"This morning, I caught a colourful bug in the garden. I wanted to put it in a box and found that matchbox with only one stick. So, I threw the matchstick and kept the bug inside the box and took it to my room. I wanted to tell Mamayya, but by the time I came out, both of you were fighting and I got scared. Sorry, all this happened because of me", said Krishna with a sad face.

"Arrey, you silly boy, said Shanta, who overheard him talking to Lakshmi.

You don't feel bad. You are not responsible for our fight. You see, after 40 years of marriage and living together, we don't need any rhyme or reason to fight.

No need of a matchbox or matchstick, fire rises just like that and douses also on its own. As you are too small to understand, just chill.

Let your Mamayya come from the office and we will all go out for a pizza, okay? Let me call him on his mobile." So saying, Shanta walked into her bedroom.

Lakshmi laughed at the dumbfounded Krishna!

3

DOUBTESHWARI

I took a sip of coffee and opened the newspaper to check what had happened around the world when I was asleep!

The front page had a picture of a smart looking woman of Indian origin, receiving a much coveted award from the chief of staff, NASA. The smile of that lady looked very familiar. I looked at her picture very closely. A saree clad lady with cropped salt and pepper hair and a small bindi, dimpled cheeks with a smile reaching her eyes. I knew her well, I mused staring at the picture.

I then looked at the caption to check the name and there it was, Dr.A.Parameshwari,

Astrophysicist. I gave out a shout so loud that I startled my husband who dropped the book he was reading!

She has done it! Oh my God! What an achievement!

I immediately ran inside to pull out my school magazine from the cupboard and flipped the pages and finally found the school day picture of my 10th standard with our class teacher. There she was with the same smile, looking into the camera, standing in the same row with me, Parameshwari, whom we had fondly nicknamed 'Doubteshwari'! She used to find something different and had doubts in anything and everything!

She exasperated all of us, including the teachers with her volley of questions. Parameshwari's why's and where's made her an enemy to all our teachers who were unable to answer most of her out of the syllabus questions. They shouted at her and sometimes even sent her out of the class for disturbing it. But that didn't deter her. During our school days in the eighties, there were no internet and google, so she spent many hours in the school library to find answers to her questions. Later, she found an ally in our new science teacher, who was doing his M.Phil, who took her to the University library to do some more research. She passed her 10th exams with a distinction and took science stream. After that, I lost touch with all my classmates as we moved away from the city with my father's transfer.

Now, after more than three decades, seeing her picture as an eminent scientist filled my heart with pride. Coming from a sleepy little town where, to be frank, she was always demotivated and ridiculed by all of us, she, with grit and determination, reached such great heights.

I saluted and wished her luck from the bottom of my heart.

Wishing my country to produce many such 'Doubteshwaris'!

4

COFFEE WITH MOTHER IN LAW

"Hey, mom is coming this weekend" shouted my husband, who was going to meet her after two long years. I was also happy, but a bit scared as well. My wedding was a whirlwind affair. It was like "He came, he saw and he married". Mihir came from Kenya on a month's leave just to marry and so it happened very quickly and before I even met his family properly, we were in Nairobi. And now I was going to meet my mil and she was going to be here for 6 months! "So happy, Mihir!" I hugged him, while sending a silent prayer to the Almighty.

I was told by Mihir, that my mil loved her coffee but it had to be exact to her set standard and that was one sure and royal way to her heart. The specifications he had given were that the coffee decoction should be thick and dark like my kaajal and milk should be very hot just like me with a dash of sugar like my sarcastic wit!

Kenya is famous for its coffee, all over the world and it's their major commercial crop. So, I thought I was all set to woo my mil with that perfect cup of coffee. But when I casually mentioned that to my friends, a bomb exploded in my head! Chicory, which is usually mixed with coffee to make it strong, was not available there and without which the coffee would be very light and not at all suitable to our South Indian palate! I was oblivious to that fact!

In a span of few hours, I saw all my dreams of impressing my mil drowning in a light tasteless coffee!

I drink only tea and Mihir was okay with anything, so I never bothered to buy coffee till now. But I learnt that all my friends, especially the ones with in laws staying with them bring chicory from India. But no one was prepared to offer me any, as it was as precious as diamond there.

No chance of asking my mil to get some chicory, because she was coming from another African country, Zambia, where my brother in law was working. I didn't want to ask my co-sister for help and degrade myself. Pride of the new bride! So, I diligently started my research to make good coffee. I searched all the stores selling coffee. Read all the labels to find any traces of chicory, but failed. Lots of coffee from Ethiopia to Jamaica, Tanzania to Uganda, but just pure coffee. Both my patience and time were running out and finally, I spotted a packet from South Africa and eagerly searched the label. I blinked my eyes in disbelief! I read it again,

Mix of Coffee n chicory!! That was a Eureka moment and I did a jig in the aisle of the shop. I came out of the shop armed with three packets of coffee and went home victorious.

My happiness was short lived. When I called my friends and announced about my discovery triumphantly, they just laughed and said that the 40 to 60 ratio of coffee to chicory is unpalatable and bitter like poison. They had tried and dumped it in the dustbin. It had to be 80 - 20 ratio to taste good, I was told. I was close to tears by the time I kept the phone down. My only hope was also dashed to the ground.

I wiped my tears and decided to face the situation head on as I remembered that I have only one day to achieve my goal of impressing my mil with her favourite cup of coffee.

I measured the pure coffee and added some of South African coffee and gave a whip in the grinder to mix the two powders well. The aim was to achieve the powder with 80:20 ratio. After that, I brewed a cup of coffee and gave it to my Good Samaritan husband to taste. He spat it after taking one sip and made a face. This coffee tasting went on for a few hours and inbetween, I offered some fried nuts and crisps as palate cleansers, in reality, bribes to Mihir for his support. After many trials and errors, I finally managed a perfect mix and the aroma n taste of the coffee was approved by

Mihir. I gave a loud cry and immediately noted the readings of my experiment in my cookery book for future reference and packed the precious coffee into a tin.

Finally, the D-day arrived and we received my mil at the airport. Before leaving for the airport I kept everything ready in the kitchen. After a warm welcome at the airport, we drove back to our home. Mihir and my mil were chatting excitedly and I sat with my heart in my mouth. We reached home and as she settled in her room, I ran to the kitchen to prepare coffee. I could still hear their animated chat, but I blocked everything from my mind and concentrated on the task at hand. I boiled the milk while stirring it continuously till it was thick and frothy.

My coffee machine chimed saying the decoction was ready. I mixed them expertly with just a dash of sugar and took the cup to my mother in law with nervous hands. She took a big sip and said "oh, coffee is good. So, chicory is available here", she quipped and then handed me a packet saying "Radha sent these chicory sachets from her stock. She carries them from Chennai for my sake. You can mix in 1 kg coffee powder with one sachet of this chicory", oblivion of my fragile condition.

The whole story of how I managed to get that correct proportion, the pain and the dedication, the amount of work that went into making her a good cup of coffee, I wanted to share, just died on my lips. I gave a weak smile and took the wretched chicory sachets from her hands and went back to the kitchen avoiding the sympathetic looks from Mihir.

That was my bitter coffee episode but now down the memory lane, it turned into a sweet memory of an innocent bride trying to win over her mil with her favourite cuppa. This aroma will never fade but will engulf me umpteen times in my life, I am sure!

5

REFLECTION

"Be careful in your new home. Don't trust your mother in law or that sweet talking sister in law of yours. You have to be very careful with these people. They will show their true colours in few days. Just listen to and then ignore all their suggestions and advises. Keep your eyes and ears open. From day one, keep a tight rein on your hubby. Don't allow him to discuss your future plans with them. They will try to make a fool of you in front of all, just to shatter your confidence. It starts from day one of your entering their home. Stay alert all the time and don't give into their sweet talk".

The monologue of Ramanamma was going on and on. Shreya was getting confused and also irritated with her mother's bashing of her in law's family. Rashmi aunty is so affectionate and her daughter Sangeeta is also very nice and she her classmate too.

She met Raman through Sangeeta and their love blossomed and this marriage happened only because of her. Sangeeta always helped them in their clandestine meetings by passing the messages/letters to each other without rousing their parents' suspicion. After all this, why is Amma scaring me like this? Shreya just wondered and was annoyed.

Shreya arrived at Raman's house in a bedecked car and entered her new home following the rituals. The house was full of Raman's relatives, all eagerly waiting for the bride and to taste and judge her culinary expertise. As a new bride, Shreya was to make a sweet dish on her first day at her new home. With her mother's warning of sabotage ringing in her ears, she slowly took steps towards the kitchen, wondering "now what"? As she was a newbie to the kitchen and entered it only to inhale the flavours of her mother's cooking. Eating was her favourite job, but, cooking.no way! Her head started whirring and suddenly she felt a soft touch on her shoulder. She looked up in alarm only to encounter a friendly smiling face of Sangeeta. "Don't look so worried dear. I know you hate cooking and same with me and Amma. Order your favourite sweet on Swiggy and chill. This is just a formality to make the new bride comfortable with her new family, not to frighten her. Amma herself sent me to reassure you. We have to show the relatives some action, so let us make some noise in the kitchen, winked Sangeeta and pulled her into the kitchen. She kept a kadai on the stove and poured some ghee. Let it smoke and you chill" gushed Sangeeta.

The Gulab Jamoons were served piping hot with cold Rabdi ordered from Gangotri restaurant in silver bowls, sprinkled with some nuts diced in the kitchen by Shreya. Everone congratulated the new bride, enjoyed the sweet dish and heaped praises on her. After that, all the guests left, Shreya hugged her mother in law and Sangeeta and thanked them wholeheartedly. This is my home, my sweet home, thought Shreya.

Later in her room alone, Shreya sat thinking about her mother. She doesn't get along with any relatives and hardly has any friends. Her suspicions and mistrust earned her more enemies than friends. Though a nice person, her habit of suspecting an ulterior motive behind everyone's action led to this, reflected Shreya. A motherless child, she was brought up by her grandmother and Attha(maternal aunt). Both of them had suffered atrocities in the hands of their respective mothers in law and others in their huge joint family. This made them very cynical and suspicious

about family members. They transferred all their anxieties and cynicism to her mother. Luckily for her, her grandmother and cousins kept in touch with her and she had a good relationship with all of them, though she met them rarely due to her mother's nature. Her father nurtured her with affection and always tried to do his best to make her a sensible being with good understanding of people. All this helped Shreya to understand her mother better and have patience with her. Still, sometimes it got too much for her to handle. Shreya was deep in her reflection about her mother.

Hey love! She suddenly jumped out of her reverie and smiled at Raman who jumped on to the bed to hug her. She looked at their reflection in the dressing mirror opposite to the bed and sighed, hoping her mother will see her family and will change her attitude. She promised to herself that with the help of her new family, she will pull her mother out of her cynicism and make her to love people and live happily. She hugged her hubby tight, to his delight .

6

LOVE IS IN THE AIR

"Amma, I am going to Sheela's house and will be back in the evening. Will have lunch there. Ok, bye", said Ramya, while reversing her scooter. "Drive slowly and be careful. Come early", replied Vani, who was having coffee with their neighbour while chit chatting.

Sundari, her neighbour, looked at Ramya going out of the building and enquired, "What is Ramie doing now? She has done her Masters, isn't it? Are you looking for alliances?"

"Yes, but not finding any. Some want a fair girl and some want a working girl. Ramya says, give me some time as she is now preparing for competitive exams and applying for private jobs as well. She is very hard working as you know! She has learnt music and she also paints beautifully. She loves cooking and experiments with new dishes. She takes part in many voluntary social activities. As it is, from tomorrow, Sheela is having exams. She is blind and Ramya helps her by volunteering as a scribe during the exams. Today, she going there so that she can familiarise herself with the syllabus and other things".

"So sweet", gushed Sundari. Really commendable work! She looked very impressed and Vani's heart swelled with pride. 'That is my Ramya', she said, with a beaming face.

"You are back! Have a wash and come quickly. I made ginger tea and onion pakora", called out Vani as soon as she saw Ramya parking her scooter in the front yard.

Ramya came in with a sweet box and said "amma, here, have some sweet.

Sheela got a job offer from the united cooperative bank. So she gave this".

Oh, but she is just a graduate, mused Vani. Yes, I too applied for the same, but she got it under the differently abled quota. I am sure she is going to ace in these PG exams too with this additional motivation", declared Ramya, munching on the kaju katli and went inside humming "apna din aayega"....!

The next morning, Ramya was having breakfast while checking her phone, Vani came and pulled another chair to sit. "Is it necessary that you waste 10 days for someone instead of preparing well for your tests? Every day, driving 20 kms to the centre to write papers for someone else, coming back tired and not having mood to study! Tell her to find someone who is free. Why can't somebody from her family help her? She is your schoolmate, I agree, but you had helped her with her graduation, isn't it? That's enough. Now, you become responsible for self" advised Vani, looking impatiently at her daughter. "Amma, what is this? Why are you talking like this? You are the one who taught me all these values of friendship, empathy, helping and respecting others! You yourself do all these things and today you are asking me to let down my friend? Till yesterday, you were fine. What happened so suddenly that you have changed your mind? Tell me ma, come on. Bring it out, please", pleaded an astonished Ramya.

"Why do you need to go and help her? She even got a job. Start thinking about self. You need to get a job so that you can get married. How long will you waste your time for others? Time to get selfish", argued a visibly frustrated Vani.

Ramya laughed loudly and said "amma, you are jealous of Sheela for getting a job!! Really!

Please ma, poor thing, she suffered so much. Her own brother always felt neglected as their parents gave more attention to Sheela due to her condition. His hatred for her grew to such an extent that he cheated her being her scribe by not writing the answers she dictated. Instead, he answered only few and left others blank making sure that she gets just pass marks and not a distinction. Only when he saw her crying profusely and had decided to apply for the recount of papers, he confessed to his sin, out of guilt.

Only after that incident, I started helping her as she failed in one of the subjects, thanks to her brother's treachery. Though interested and capable, she couldn't take part in many activities as our schools didn't have facilities needed for differently abled students. Even teachers are not trained to deal with such students' emotional anxiety and physical problems. Inspite of all these drawbacks, few like Sheela are shining because of people like you who taught their children about inclusiveness and who are ready to take responsibility of others if and when needed. Amma, I am so proud to be your daughter! I know you are upset as another rejection came from the boy's family and you are worried about my future. As long as you and naanna are with me, I don't care what society says about my colour. I want to marry a person who likes me as I am, with all my strengths and faults. Don't worry, the lucky guy is lurking somewhere and will jump out suddenly, you see" and she jumped to follow her words and Vani laughed at her antics and said "sorry! Very stupid of me, but I got really upset by their call. Anyway, let's move on." Vani went in and came out of the kitchen with a box and water bottle. "Here, take this box with a few cake pieces for both of you. My best wishes to Sheela". She sent Ramya wholeheartedly and scolded herself for being so negative for a moment. "Srinivasa, give me strength to be a good human", she prayed to her lord of seven hills.

Ramya entered home shouting "amma tea, I am famished, but so happy. Today's paper went well. Sheela prepared really well". She came out of her room after a wash to see Sundari aunty entering the house. She went and greeted her as usual. Sundari, after exchanging a few pleasantries, gave an envelope to Ramya. "I always admired your qualities and the confidence with which you carry out all your activities. My nephew is also looking for a life partner. So, with your mother's permission, I had sent your photo and other details. He sent his details and asked me to handover it to you. So, now you both decide the future course of action. Best wishes". She wished Ramya and went to chat with Vani.

Ramya walked into her room with tea in one hand and an envelope in another. She settled in her favourite nook, took a big sip of tea and then opened the envelope.

A colour photo slipped out and a fair, normal built guy with glasses smiled at her. She looked at it for few minutes trying to assess and then opened the letter.

Hi Ramya Garu,

I am Teja from Mumbai. I am a banker working in a multinational bank.

Fair, small built and a very normal guy with simple ambitions.

I enjoy reading, listening to music and of course, am a film buff.

Nothing spectacular about me.

I heard about up you from Sundari pinni.

In my family of four, all are fair but that's just because of our DNA and we are petty casual about it. So you being dark, is not even an issue.

My wife working or non-working, I leave it to her and the circumstances.

If and when need arises it will be resolved, is my opinion. Can't foresee the future.

I enjoy being social and do help people but am not a volunteer or anything.

To be frank, I never ever thought about it. Shocking, isn't it!

Our ideas may match or you may find me boring or listless!

So, let's find out! If it's ok with you and your family, we can connect on phone/mails to know more about each other and our families too, as I feel they are an integral part of any marriage.

If our ideas match and we like each other, we will then take the next step.

Otherwise, we can be friends at least! What do you say?

If you are ok, do call or give missed call on the number given below. If not, it's okay.

With warm regards,

Tejaswi.

Folding the letter, Ramya felt warmth spreading through her body.

So there are still people, who believe in giving girls their due, respect their feelings and look beyond the skin colour, not blinded or bound by society's illogic!

Yes, she entered the number into her mobile.

With a big smile on her face, she reclined on her bed looking at the full moon peeping into her room through the open window and started singing her all-time favourite

"Ye zindagi usiki hai jo kisika ho gaya"..............!

HOME SWEET HOME

I am in love with my new home. Big garden to roam with plenty of flowers and fruit bearing trees. Big gated house and fence to stop stray animals from entering. Airy rooms with plenty of cupboards and big attics. Best of all, the lady of the house is a busy entrepreneur and kids are studying abroad.

So, it's quite empty and gives me lot of freedom to move around without anyone's interference. Another good thing about this house is, there are no pets. I don't mind few fish in an aquarium or love birds or parrots in a cage. But being a foodie, sometimes I do wonder how well they may taste if cooked well! Dogs also I tolerate, they don't bother me much. But cats, yuk, I can't stand them. They are not loyal or useful like dogs. Waste of owner's time and money, I feel.

As my owner and the lady are busy people, the running of the house is left to the servants. The house is managed by Gowri the cook cum maid. Gowri loves cooking, watching TV and chatting on phone. She cooks lovely food and keeps it on the kitchen platform to cool, while continuously talking on phone. Most of the time she forgets to cover or covers it partially. Then she plops on a sofa in the living room glued to the TV. The wonderful aroma of the food pulls me out of my cosy corner and I stealthily enter the kitchen to take one bite of this and one of that without her notice. I love her paneer tikka, samosas, and bread cutlet, actually everything. Her gajar ka halwa is so yummy, I make many trips to the kitchen, while she is engrossed in the TV. Once the food items are cool, she will pack them in containers and then they are out of my reach. I had to take my chance before that.

Today, the smell of something deep fried woke me from my slumber. I quickly rubbed my eyes and slowly sauntered towards the kitchen. I was about to enter it but then suddenly stopped in my tracks at the sight of the big cat with a shiny coat and a collar around its neck. I ran back with that cat running behind me like Yama. I leaped into my hole in the backyard but can hear that wretched cat scratching the ground and growling in anger. Time to look for another home, I thought sadly. Going to miss this home, especially Gowri's food.

SPECTRUM OF LIFE

Year 1960.........

Savitri was busy scribbling in her notebook. A new idea just came to her mind and she was eagerly penning it in her book lest she may forget the plot. Her story was progressing well except for few smudges of soot from her fingers. Suddenly, the smell of burning rice filled her nostrils. She hurriedly dropped her book and ran into the kitchen situated at the end of the main house. She quickly took the tongs and removed the pot from the stove and checked the inside of the pot. The rice inside had turned black like coal and the burnt smell filled the air and she started coughing and her eyes started streaming with tears from both smoke and grief. The coal was burning red in the stove and her mother in law's face was also equally red with anger. Savitri shrieked in terror as her mother in law slapped her hard on her cheek which immediately turned the same bright red.

"Donga gaadidha (Thief donkey)! She hit her with the rope in her hand "How many times had I told you not to leave the kitchen while cooking? But you never listen. I made a mistake of getting a literate daughter in law and am now suffering. You were again either reading or writing some stupid story, isn't it? My warnings were not enough for you! Now just wait and watch. I know how to teach you a lesson"!

Lakshmamma angrily walked into the room and grabbed all the novels and books from the cupboard including Savitri's writing book and entered the kitchen and to Savitri's horror, dropped all of them into the brightly burning stove. The fire leapt high and engulfed all the books hungrily. That was the end of Savitri's dream of becoming a writer. Her dream was burnt to ashes along with her books.

Year 1990........

"Today again rice with leftovers from morning meal", grumbled Sivaram, dropping the lid of sambar with a loud clatter, dissatisfaction written large on his face.

"Ofcourse your wife is busy writing stories. Madam is now a big famous writer!

Chesukunnavuga, anubhavinchu (you had chosen her, suffer)", commented Radha, eating her hot upma prepared by the same famous writer.

Latha looked up from the typewriter guiltily and said "sorry, but the deadline is in two days for the novel competition by the prestigious Yuva Publication. Almost done, just a few corrections. I am absolutely free from tomorrow after I post it. Just adjust for one day", she pleaded with her husband. Sivaram stomped away to the bedroom. In a few minutes, he came out fully dressed and took his scooter keys and said I am going out for dinner. You finish your work happily! Husband and his comforts are not your priority. The success went to your head. You don't need me. Do whatever you want", he slammed the door and left.

Latha got up from the table with tears and went to look at her kids sleeping in their room. She stood looking at their innocent faces. They are the only solace in her life.

She writes novels about love, sacrifices and sweet endings while her own life is miserable. Except for the twins, there is nothing in her life. No joy. Her mother in-law's irk, she can understand, but her husband, inspite of being highly educated, is no better than her illiterate mother in law. He always finds faults and never supports or lends a helping hand, but enjoys the fruits of her labour. The scooter was bought by her earnings as a writer. He is jealous of her fame and insults her in front of their friends just to show that he is the boss of the house. The mangalsutram (nuptial chain) in her neck is like a noose to her now. She controlled her sobs and left the room quietly to finish her novel titled 'Prema Vijayam' (Triumph of love)!!!!

Year 2020

The Ravindra Bharthi auditorium was fully packed with book lovers and filmi buffs. Miss. Maya is a very popular novelist and a successful film director. Many of her books were turned into blockbuster movies. All her protagonists are women with deep convictions and strength of character. Top heroines vie with each other to get that all important role in her films.

All her novels and movies were also criticality acclaimed for their sensitivity and many layered portrayal of women. Today, she is being felicitated by the Andhra Pradesh Government with the Nandi award for best story writer/ director for the super success movie 'Swapnalu'(Dreams).

After the felicitation, there was an interaction session with the media. Many journalists from popular television channels were present. Many questions were posed about the film, the cast and the making of the film and the challenges faced. One journalist wanted to know the reason for her being still single in spite of many proposals from many successful suitors.

Maya replied "to be able to live and work in peace. You know, my granny Savitri Devi always wanted to be a writer and she was also very good at it. I read a few of her stories written on the back of old receipts and shoved inside her trunk concealed

from her mother in-law. Her family never supported her but instead, punished her for her dream. She died without fulfilling her dream. But she passed that dream to her daughter and my mother.

I am the daughter of the well-known novelist Latha, who wrote super romantic novels while mentally being tortured by her husband and mother in law. She died of disappointment and heartache. I was young at that time, but understood how lonely she felt in spite of having a husband and family. Her husband valued her money but treated her like dirt.

He never lifted a finger to help her physically or adjusted to her busy schedule. She had to finish all her chores, take care of kids and then find time to pursue her passion of writing. He certainly enjoyed the fruits of her passion but his male ego stopped him from either praising her or respecting her in public. He enjoyed publicly humiliating her to stroke his ego. She was like a puppet which moved the way he pulled the ropes! The mental agony and torture killed her prematurely with a heart attack when I was still in school.

So only, I decided to stay strong and alone to fight injustice towards women and make them mentally strong through my writings and movies. I am against society's norm which says women are complete only after marriage and kids. I strongly believe that we are complete on our own and happy too. Marriage and kids are optional, not necessary or mandatory. It's an individual's choice and need. We don't need props to make us successful in life. I want to prove that by leading such a life.

I am not saying all men are alike, but unfortunately, majority are like that. The saddest part is that it's usually women against a woman. As a mother in law or daughter in law, we instigate men against our own. The situation has not changed much from my grandmother's time. We all have to change the society by coming together, working together and breaking the glass ceiling. We have to make it better for the future generations. I am and will strive for it". With that, she folded her hands in namaste and took leave from the media and left the auditorium with her head high and a beautiful smile on her radiant face.

9

COMPASSION

Sarala was looking at the ceiling, lost in her thoughts. The octogenarian woke up at 5 AM as usual but with nothing to do or look forward to, spent her time in bed till 7 AM thinking about the past and her routine during earlier years which now felt like was another life time. Finally, grumbling, she got up from the bed and with the help of her tripod walking stick, walked slowly into the bathroom with all the amenities required for the elderly fitted by her son Shankar. After finishing her morning routine, she walked into the kitchen and made herself a cup of coffee and took 2 biscuits from the tin kept next to the coffee maker presented by her daughter in-law Janaki. She slowly made her way to the balcony and sat there sipping her coffee and looking at her plants in full bloom in the small garden, managed efficiently by her gardener, Bola. He was getting regular instructions on video calls from Shankar who loved plants and was an expert in gardening. Organic vegetables for his mother from the kitchen garden and fresh flowers for her morning puja were all managed through these tutorials. Even her cook Kamakshi got tips on healthy and tasty cooking from both Shankar and Janaki.

They both tried to make her happy by taking care of all her needs and were available always to talk to her. But Sarala was still unhappy as they had not moved back to India to be with her in her twilight years. Yes, they took them to London when her husband was diagnosed with cancer and provided the best available treatment and the much needed physical and emotional support.

After his death, they wanted her to stay with them. But with her grandson in boarding school, both her son and daughter in law at work, she was alone and bored at home. She also missed her home, her routine and her mother land. So, after six months of stay, she decided to come back to her home in Hyderabad. For a few years, she enjoyed her life of living alone, visiting friends and family, going to temples, meeting her friends for lunches and movies. But slowly, her energy levels dipped and with age, her going out also reduced. Most of her friends were also in the same situation and moved to be with their children or were managing with helpers. All were home bound and in touch mostly on WhatsApp or calls. They meet very rarely now, may be twice or thrice in a year for some special occasion.

The morning puja was done and Sarala sat at the dining table for breakfast to be served by Kamakshi as her mobile rang. It was her son's morning call. She ignored it, concentrating on her oat idli and tomato chutney. After sometime, she heard Kamisha talking to Shankar and updating him regarding her health and other activities. Sarala just walked into the living room and stood in front of the book shelf. She took a few books out, dusted and kept them back. She looked at the photographs on the wall. Shankar as a kid on a tricycle, his graduation picture, his wedding picture with Janaki, her grandson in her hands kissing her cheek, her husband's garlanded picture.... She took one wet cloth and cleaned all the pictures of dust and arranged them properly. She sat on a corner sofa to read and then the doorbell chimed. Kamakshi went to open the door and yelled in surprise! Chinnababu! (Little one)

Yes! Shouted back Ravi. Sarala was too shocked to utter any word.

She stared her grandson without blinking. Ravi moved closer to hug her and said "I had to fly to meet you and see what's going on. You are on non-cooperation movement with amma and naanna (mother n father). Not answering their calls, not replying to messages. They were so worried, I decided to find out personally and took the first flight. But now, I will go and have my shower and

Kamakshi akka (elder sister), keep one hot and strong coffee ready please". He dashed into the guest room with his backpack.

Ravi sprawled on the settee with his feet on a pile of cushions complaining of swollen feet. He assured a worried Sarala that it's common for him after a long flight with little leg space. He joked with Sarala, "baamma (Grandma), I am also getting old. I am now thirty, so all these pains are ok. Naanna has high blood pressure due to the pressures of his work and amma is diabetic, a genetic disorder. Both are managing with exercise, diet and medication. Apart from their work tensions, recently they were worried about you and it's showing on their health. That's the reason I took a direct flight of 14 hours to come here though I knew it was going to give me some trouble. No worries, as by tomorrow, I will be all good". Sarala felt a twinge of guilt as she never knew about her son and daughter in law's health issues. She was always complaining about herself but never thought about them.

While having lunch, Ravi casually asked Sarala, "baamma, why don't you move to London to be with naanna. He feels guilty that you are alone here without any family.

You can stay there and they will be happy to be around you in your old age. You can go out to temples, malls and restaurants with them. Watch T.V like you do here. We even get Indian channels. You can buy books online, chat with your friends on phone. You won't miss anything. Of course they go to office, but are back by evening and weekends, they are absolutely free. I also stay close by with my girlfriend. We also visit you" his monologue was cut short by Sarala's curt reply "it's difficult for me to adjust at this age. Why can't they move back? They made enough money and worked enough. Why can't they move here to our ancestral house? Is it not his responsibility to look after me in this last few years? "Her voice choked with tears.

Ravi smiled at her and said "baamma, you and thaatha wanted naanna to go abroad to study as it was a prestige in those days. He found a job and sent money so you can build this house and get other amenities. Even when thaatha got sick, they managed to provide good health care and other facilities with their earnings. They became citizens and I was born there. They struggled, worked hard to build their whole life there. We have our jobs, friends and memories. We have more attachment to that alien land which became our motherland now. You can't expect us to tear away everything and come back here. It's one person against three persons' lives. Is it fair? We are always thinking about your comfort and happiness. Is it not fair that you too should think about us and our life? Even naanna is now 62 years old and amma almost sixty. They took care of you for the past 20 years coming down whenever there was a medical emergency or you were feeling lonely and depressed. But now, they also need the same support from me. If you move there, you can actually make their life simple and easy to manage. Here, you are alone all the time, whereas they are away only for a few hours and also just a phone call away. This is your motherland but you are a mother and have a chance to prove that you care for the children. This argument of yours "I can't adjust at this age doesn't hold water. What is so difficult for you? You are not anyway able to go out and do all the things you used to do. You don't have any responsibilities to tie you down to this place. The climate, cold are just your pretexts to avoid coming there. Our house is heated and you can comfortably set the temperature to your liking. Whenever you go out, car, shopping malls, restaurants are all with heating facilities. You just have to make up your mind and be positive to move and stay with your son. Why does your generation always emotionally blackmail children saying we sacrificed everything for you and you never reciprocated? Do you have any idea how much guilty naanna is feeling because of your accusations?

You just made all his efforts for you and thaatha nothing and they have no value. How painful it was for him, did you realise? And then, he suddenly looked up to see a visibly shaken Sarala and stopped. He went to her and apologised, "sorry baamma, if I had hurt you with my tirade, but I just want you to know that it's easy to blame your kids but difficult to adjust and lead life. Anyway, I decided to stay here with you and take care of you. I will work from here as my work hours are flexible. It's good for all of us and less stress". He hugged his granny and went out, leaving Sarada to her own thoughts.

Kamakshi sighed listening to all this. Sometimes parents become so selfish that they don't even realise that they are hurting their kids and killing the relationship. Luckily for Saralamma, her family are very sincere and loving. "God bless" them, prayed Kamakshi, thinking of Shankar and family.

10

DANCE LIKE NO ONE'S WATCHING

The house was full with relatives from both sides of the family. Almost all the family and Ramya's friends were arriving to pay last respects to her grandmother. Her grandmother, Laksmi was bedecked in her favourite Kanjeevaram saree, big red bindi and not to forget, the mallepoo lovingly arranged by Ramya's grandfather himself, muttering "last time dear Laksmi, till we meet on the other side".

After the final send off and rituals of 13 days, the house was empty, except for the family. As her vacation was ending in a week, Ramya started her packing. Ramya's grandfather walked into her room and slowly lowered himself into the chair. "It was good that you were here for the last two months, your grandma had a good time before she suddenly left us all. Who thought a healthy lady of 68 will pass away so suddenly in sleep of massive heart attack?" his voice broke and tears rolled down his cheeks. He was still grappling to come to terms with his sudden loss. Ramya stopped her packing, went and sat next to him. She took his hands and tenderly asked "you want to talk about amamma. Even I want to know more about her, thaatha".

Rajaram took a long breath and said "we got married very young. I was still in college and your amamma was just 15 yrs old. She loved singing and dancing, but my parents were orthodox and they didn't allow her. Then your father and attha were born and she got busy with them. Again, she wanted at least your attha to learn dance but even that was not allowed. Also, your attha was more interested in studies and that's it. But I always watched her dancing to any song on radio when she thought no one was around. Even though I wanted her to dance, but never had the courage with my parents around. Even during our children's weddings all others danced but your amamma couldn't. By the time my parents passed away, we both got busy with you grandchildren. Even though I was aware of her desire to dance at least once, I never had the courage and now it's too late. She never asked for anything and this, I could have done, but now", he couldn't finish his sentence and started sobbing.

Ramya went and got her mobile and showed him her Instagram posts of her amamma's dance posts. Both grandmother and granddaughter were in full costume, makeup and matching accessories and were dancing to the popular dance numbers from Vijayanthimala's movies of yesteryears. "Thaatha, remember last month you all went to attend a family function and I said I am not well and amamma stayed back to look after me? We planned the whole thing that time. You all went out and then, my friends came over and we did the whole shoot in those two days. Amamma not only picked up all her dance steps in one day, she also did the whole shoot in just under 2 hours, which even my friend, who taught us the dance, thought was amazing. We shared it on Instagram and uploaded it on YouTube. It created a storm on the Internet, with over a million views and thousands of shares. People loved her dance and her zeal. All my friends became her fans. All this just before she passed away suddenly. We were lucky as none of you are interested in social media, and those who are, were tight lipped, knowing our bereavement. Amamma was planning to surprise you and also confess to you about her crime, but she never got a chance. Hope you are not angry with us. I just wanted to fulfill her dream of dancing" said Ramya.

Rajaram hugged her with all his strength and said, "angry? No dear, I am so happy and proud of you that you got her wish fulfilled and that too in such a beautiful and grand way! Now I am so happy knowing that my Lakshmi finally got a chance and danced to her heart's content. I don't want anything more in this life. Stay blessed, my dear. You did what none of us even never thought of doing". Both Ramya and Rajaram went out to share Lakshmi's dance debut with others.

11

ANONYMOUS LETTER

'Jaanu, jaanu', Kishore's voice from the bedroom brought a happy smile to Archana's face who was busy preparing breakfast in the kitchen. She took a hand towel to wipe her hands clean and adjusted her bindi. She peeped into the ornate mirror hung on the corridor wall to check her kaajal and hair before stepping into the bedroom. Kishore was sitting cross legged on the bed with his eyes closed, like a sage meditating. Archana went and stood in front of him like an apsara and said 'good morning'. Kishore opened his eyes and looked lovingly into her eyes and said 'love you, jaanu'. Now my day begins', and with a smile, went into the bathroom to start his daily routine.

Archana went back to the kitchen thinking how lucky she was! Even after two years of marriage this morning routine has not changed. On their wedding night, Kishore asked her to promise that everyday, she will be there when he wakes up and she should be the first sight of his day. And to this day, it is the ritual, except when he was out of station on business tour. Those days, he manages by looking at her photo, which he always kept in his wallet. Her heart was filled with love and was bulging with happiness, just like the pooris she was deep frying for their breakfast. She arranged the table with pooris and potato curry, fruit and fresh juice, the way Kishore likes. Coffee was brewing in the machine and the delicious smell of fresh brew wafted through the kitchen. Archana sat at the table, day dreaming till the fragrance of Kishore's deodorant tickled her nostrils. Smartly dressed and carrying his jacket, Kishore came to the table exclaiming 'my favourite breakfast ! Oh, today, your cheat day!! Good for me'. He winked at Archana and pulled his chair and joined her at the table. Kishore finished his breakfast and got up to leave. He kissed Archana on her cheek as she was still munching on her poori, waved bye and left for his office.

Archana sat with her cup of coffee and the newspaper. She was busy reading it when the bell rang and Archana went to open the door. Satya, her maid was standing with an envelope in her hand. She greeted Archana and said 'madam, I found it on the door mat', handed it to her and went inside. Archana was puzzled. A letter, that too lying on the mat! She looked at the plain white envelope addressed to her. No sender's address or stamps. With consternation, she opened the envelope to see a typed letter. As she read the short note, her heartbeat quickened and she started sweating profusely. She felt like fainting and kept the letter down. She asked Satya to get her some water and took big gulps to steady herself. After recovering from the initial shock, she took the letter and started reading again slowly to digest the unpleasant news.

Dear Madam,

You are being fooled by your husband Mr. Kishore Verma.

He is having a roaring affair for the past few years with one Maya memsaheb.

He is very cunning and covers his tracks well.

Take off your blinders and see the real picture!

Your anonymous friend and well-wisher.

Archana's head was spinning and her body went numb. She stared into the letter and sat like a rock. She came out of her reverie with Satya's call, 'madam your kichdi is ready. Shall I set the table for your lunch?. She lost her appetite and all she wanted was to curl up in bed and forget all about this unpleasant letter. Archana snapped at her, saying 'no need'. You just leave, I am not feeling well, I am going to rest'. With that, she sent Satya away, locked the main door and went into the bedroom. There, she sat looking into the letter and tried recollecting any Maya either in Kishore's office or in his friends' circle. The name did not ring a bell at all. She had never met anyone with that name, and she was very sure of it. She thought of calling him up on his mobile, but decided against it. Time was ticking away, but she stayed in her bed, looking at the ceiling, while agonising thoughts pierced her heart.

Kishore parked his car in the portico and noticed that the house was dark except the light in the verandah. He quickly climbed the stairs and saw the main door was ajar and Archana sitting in the hall in complete darkness. He pushed the door open and enquired 'what happened ? No electricity? What about the inverter?

He then said, but the verandah and portico lights are working?'

Who is Maya? From how long this has been going on behind my back? The questions came out like bullets and Kishore stopped in his tracks. He thanked the darkness as he tried to control the shock and fear showing on his face. 'What dear? Who is this Maya? What is all this?' His voice came out hoarsely. His mind was racing with thoughts, 'how is this possible?' No one knows about this even in the office. I always took care to meet her only outside Hyderabad. We booked our flight tickets also separate. Never went to the same hotel twice to avoid recognition. Then how, how? Of all the people, how Archana got this news. His head was splitting with all kinds of questions and then suddenly, he heard Archana laughing loud and the lights came on.

Archana stood there in a dazzling red chiffon saree with subtlety applied makeup and matching accessories. Looking at his astonished face, she smiled and said 'sorry dear, this year, I fooled you! April fool banaya! Remember last year you kept that wretched plastic lizard on the kitchen platform and I screamed my head off and almost fainted, while you happily sang 'April fool banaya!! This year too, you have almost succeeded. I got the letter and the whole afternoon, I was miserable with all kind of stupid thoughts. I even missed my lunch. But then suddenly, I saw the bedside calendar and then realised that it's April first and this was your prank. I know how much you love me. You can't terrify me with a stupid anonymous letter, ok?' And what a name, Maya!! All your maya, Narada muni! Now for this nautanki, you are taking me out on a long drive and dinner. So, hurry up, she smiled triumphantly at Kishore and blew a flying kiss.

Recovering from his shock, Kishore showed his disappointment with a sad face and said 'my darling, difficult to beat you! Thought I planned it well and it was foolproof. But no chance with you! Okay, give me a few minutes to freshen up' and he hurried to the bathroom with a poker face.

Kishore closed the door and wiped the sweat from his face and took a few deep breaths and thanked his stars. It was a close shave and for a moment, he thought his affair with Maya was out in the open. He immediately picked up his mobile to alert Maya.

He met Maya few years ago before his marriage. A freelance photographer and a writer, she doesn't believe in the institution of marriage and preferred an informal relationship. Both used to meet regularly, but decided to end their relationship after his marriage. But as luck would have it, Archana hates travel and preferred staying at home during Kishore's business trips. They again gave in to the temptation and continued their sojourns outside the city. Both were conscious of their reputation, so they took all the necessary steps to keep it under the wraps. Even their close friends were not aware of it. So, it was a mystery for Kishore and he was determined to find the person who wrote the letter. He immediately made a mental note to hire a private detective to find the anonymous friend first thing in the morning. Also, a few months of hibernation will be good to completely bury this anonymous friend, he decided. With all the necessary planning done, Kishore took a quick shower and got ready in a matching red shirt and jeans and his signature deodorant and looked at himself in the mirror and once again thanked his lucky stars.

Kishore stepped out of the room singing, 'mai zoru ka ghulam banke rahoonga'!!

Anonymous letter - part 2.

The bell rang and a visibly happy Archana opened the door and greeted Satya with a big smile. "Come in", she said with a smile and turned around, humming an old melody. Satya walked in slowly, asking "what madam? Today you look very happy. Yesterday I was scared because you looked so sad and upset after reading that letter". Archana sat on the sofa and replied, "oh, that was just a very bad prank from your sir. Anyway, I took a nice revenge. Dinner at a five star hotel, second show movie with popcorn and ice cream. I even did some shopping at the boutique in the hotel! Now, he will never do it again". Hahaha......laughed Archana.

Suddenly, she looked up at Satya, who was looking at her sadly with eyes filled with tears. Archana was shocked and went to Satya. 'what happened'? why are looking so glum?" she questioned. "Oh, madam. You are so innocent and nice. That is why sir is taking advantage and cheating you", replied Satya. "What? What nonsense are you talking? How dare you talk like this?" Archana went livid with anger. "Get out of my house. Don't ever come anywhere near it in the future. After all I did for you, this is what you have to say? Get out", shouted Archana. "Madam, I will go away. No problem. But first listen to what I have to say. You always helped me whenever I needed it. Always treated me well and with respect. I will never forget that. That's why when I came to know about sir and that lady, I wanted to alert you. Please believe me. I just want you to know the truth", pleaded Satya with folded hands.

Archana's head started aching with tension. She slumped into the sofa and invited Satya to sit. Satya pulled a chair to sit and took a deep breath. "Madam, you know that my son works in the airport lounge. He told me a few months ago that he saw sir with a lady. My son recognised sir as he had seen him a few times when he came to drop me on his scooter. But I didn't pay much attention. But when he said he saw them travelling together frequently and they were very intimate, I then got worried. He even took pictures of them secretly on his phone. But I didn't know how to broach the subject with you. So, my son came up with this anonymous letter idea and got one ready and gave it to me to deliver. We thought you will corner your husband with that letter and truth will come out. But it looks like he fooled you again. Madam, if you want, you can see these pictures" Satya got her phone out to show the pictures to Archana. Though she couldn't recognise the lady, the posture and their facial expressions were evident enough for Archana to understand. She just went numb with pain. How can she be so foolish? She had never suspected him. She now recalled Kishore's initial reaction of fear and his voice. But being a romantic fool, she thought it was his pain because she misunderstood him. Oh God!

She was not just a April fool, but a complete fool! Kishore must have enjoyed her stupidity yesterday! He must have had a good laugh with his memsaheb! Her stomach churned with anger and disgust. Slowly, she controlled herself, got up and hugged Satyavati. "Thank you so much. Sorry for my outburst and thanks for thinking about me and my welfare. You are my guardian angel. Now, just forward those pics to my mobile. I will straight away contact my cousin, who is a leading lawyer. So saying, she briskly went into her bedroom with her mobile in hand asking Satyavati to prepare strong coffee for both of them.

That evening, Kishore was back from office as usual to find Archana at the dining table. She gave him a perfunctory look and said, "please come and sit, I need to talk to you. He pulled a chair with a grin and said "need help with your crossword?". "No, my life is now at crossroads and I am trying to find the right way", she replied jauntily and pushed a few papers towards him. I consulted my lawyer and got the papers ready. I found out Maya's address and other details with the help of her photo and few bribes. I even met and talked to Maya and she confessed about your romantic trips. I don't have any grudge or anger against her. She is an adult and single. Not answerable to any or to be blamed.

But whereas, you are a married and a committed man. You have commitment towards me and you have failed in keeping up those promises. You cheated me by committing adultery. I was a fool but I don't want to be one for life. I have signed these papers for divorce by mutual consent. I have enough proof and witnesses to drag you to the court to punish you, but our families don't deserve all that public muck. Sign these papers after consulting your lawyer and let's part ways amicably. Kishore's facial expressions changed from shock to fear, from distress to dismay. He tried saying something, but nothing came out of his lips. He finally pleaded with folded hands to give him another chance to mend his ways.

Archana stood up and said, "second chance is given for crime committed unaware or in the heat of the moment but not for those committed knowingly and in a planned manner. No use now, as I completely lost my trust in you. This was a cold blooded murder of our relationship".

Thank you for this unforgettable lesson. With that, Archana picked up her suitcase and walked out without a backward glance.

12

INTANGIBLE

Sakshi angrily entered the staff room and went to her desk. She dropped her tiffin box and flask into the drawer and snapped it shut with a loud thud. Reshma lifted her head from the newspaper, in which her head was tucked in a few moments ago. She looked at her from top to bottom and commented "lover's tiff! Honeymoon over, already"!!"

Sakshi glared at her and walked out of the staff room still fuming. "How dare he comment on my work ! Just a teacher. I will give you that salary as pocket money, you stay home. Resign your job and manage your home! How easy for him to say that!! Before marriage, one tune and after marriage, another tune, men!!". She almost collided into Revathi walking out of her class. Hey, what's wrong? Why are you looking so angry?" She put her hand around Sakshi's shoulders and moved her towards the canteen.

Their usual two cups of tea and a plate of Marie biscuits were placed before them by Raju, the canteen boy along with two glasses of cold water. After two biscuits and a few sips of tea, Sakshi opened her heart to her bosom friend. "Every day the same topic. My job as primary teacher is below his dignity. We met only because of my job when he came to drop his friend's kid in my class. That time, it was a great job but after marriage he finds it awkward to introduce me to his friends as a school teacher. Everyday, we fight over this and it spoils my mood and is affecting my work too. I don't know how to make him understand that it's not just a job but my lifeline. It has always been my dream to mould the young into creative and confident adults and inspire them achieve their dreams. However, Vikram is not able to understand my passion and this is resulting in one big tug of war between us. My parents are also supporting him and saying I am being stubborn. As he is a CEO of a big company, it is my duty as an ideal wife to resign the job and avoid embarrassment to him.

I am feeling so helpless. Sometimes, I feel that I made a mistake of marrying him without clarifying all the issues. But I never felt that he will be so ashamed of my job.

I thought he is well read, well travelled and will appreciate what I am doing and aspiring to do. But I was mistaken". Her voice was low and she was struggling to control her tears. Revathi was shocked hearing this. She considered Vikram to be a matured, confident and understanding person. But this revelation stunned her and she felt sorry for Sakshi who was so passionate about her job and wards.

The bell rang and they both stood up to go to their respective classes. "Take it easy for a few days. Our year is ending in a week and then we are closed for two months. Try and explain to him lovingly. Don't worry, everything will be fine." Revathi tried to cheer her up and Sakshi nodded her head in agreement and then hurried to her class.

The school was very noisy with kids and their parents coming back after the long summer vacation. A few were excited to see their friends and teachers while a few were crying, not ready to leave their parents. The teachers were busy greeting and talking to them. Suddenly, Revathi saw Sakshi entering the school in a brand new car. She parked the car and came running towards Revathi with a big grin on her face. "Let's meet during the break, I have lots to tell", she whispered and went to meet her students.

Revathi spotted Sakshi sitting in the canteen and she went and sat on the chair opposite to her and said, "now tell me, quickly. I can't bear any more. New car and new you! What's the matter?" Sakshi gave a sweet smile and said "our trip to Ooty solved my problem. You know, on the flight we met the parents of my old student, who is now in 5th grade and they thanked me for turning their unruly kid into a disciplined all rounder. We met another set of parents in the hotel we stayed, where the parents insisted on paying our dinner bill just to show their gratitude for taking care of their daughter during her formative years. Vikram was so touched by their love. Finally, while we were walking in a mall, another student came running to greet me. He hugged and kissed me saying he missed me and was waiting for the school's reopening. Vikram was completely bowled over by this incident.

He said he always looked at the position, salary and other tangible things, but never understood the value of intangibles like love, affection and gratitude. He said he never experienced this as a boss and people never greeted or thanked him with so much affection. He said I taught him the value of intangibles in life and gifted me a car and said he is happy to be the husband of a primary teacher, who taught values to all, including him!!

Revathi jumped up happily and hugged her tight and shouted "Raju, two Cadbury's! Celebration time! Kuch meetha hojaye"!.

13

BEING A GIRL

Satya was looking at the cinema poster in front of the bus stop. "Walk fast, don't stare at all those heroes. Behave like a girl", chided Ramarao. Satya quickened her steps and followed her father.

"Leave that laddu for your brother. That's the last one", warned Rajeshwari. "But I also want to eat! Will keep half for him", bargained Satya. "Leave it in the box", shouted Rajeshwari. "Behave like a girl ! Go to the kitchen and eat that dosa quickly and then draw water from the well". I don't want dosa, whined Satya and the next instant, was slapped hard by her mother. Crying aloud, she went to the backyard to fill water.

Kabaddi kabaddi, Satya repeated while going around to touch one of the boys, when her teacher Malati pulled her by her plait to one side and said, "don't wear frocks hereafter, wear parikini (full skirt) to school. Also, stop playing kabaddi with boys in the school. Behave. Be a girl," lectured Satya's class teacher .

Satya was an intelligent girl with ambition and drive. Her energy and enthusiasm were boundless. She wanted to study well and become a police officer. She admired Swati Rao, the Telangana cadre IPS officer and wanted to be fierce and energetic like her. She watched her interviews on TV in the community hall and also read about her in the newspaper articles. Swati was her idol and she dreamt of becoming one like her. But her parents and teachers of her school never understood her ambition and kept her pushing to be a good homely girl. When she tried talking to her mother and teachers about her ambition, they just laughed and made fun of her saying, she is day dreaming and just because she is getting good marks doesn't mean she can reach that level. They advised her to concentrate on learning useful things like sewing and cooking instead of wasting her energy in playing games like kabaddi and badminton with boys. By such acts, she was bringing disgrace to the family, chastised the elders. Satya was hugely disappointed by the actions of her teachers. She was not expecting this from them. She thought at least her teachers will understand her dreams and support her in realising them by convincing her parents. She was lost in her thoughts and suddenly, heard Ms. Swati Rao speaking on TV about how she got into her profession against all odds with the help of an NGO and social service departments. Satya immediately noted down the name of the NGO and next morning, she wrote a detailed letter about her ambition and the hardships she was facing. She also mentioned about her idol and her talk on TV, which prompted her to write the letter to them. She attached her school certificates and other documents and posted them secretly and waited with her fingers crossed. Finally, after a month, her waiting ended and she received a letter from the NGO. She read the letter and couldn't believe her eyes. She heaved a sigh of relief and clutched the letter to her bosom.

As promised, a representative from that NGO arrived at the school and met her. After consulting the headmaster, her parents were called to the school. The representative explained that they were offering a scholarship to Satya under meritorious student category, under which her educational, lodging and boarding expenses will be borne by the organisation. This arrangement will be till her higher secondary and depending on her performance, it will continue further. After a lot of resistance, her parents finally agreed to send Satya to the city to join the school run by the NGO. Satya was on cloud nine. Packing her things and saying good bye to her family, she ran to the waiting vehicle and boarded it.

The school was all decked up to receive their alumni returning as Satya, IPS.

Satya rose from her chair to address the audience to a thunderous applause.

Her classmates and teachers were all excited to hear the story of her long journey. "Dream and dream big is my advice to all. Don't dream with your eyes closed, dream with your eyes open and work towards it. The universe will conspire and help you in realising it. There are people and institutes to help but you have to reach out with your effort. God helps only those people who help themselves. So, take action, do not just dream. I dreamt and followed it by acting upon it. I promise to help anyone who wants to achieve something in life. I am always available to you all. Let us take the name of this sleepy village to the headlines of all major newspapers by our achievements. Be a girl, but never sacrifice your dreams.

Take a pledge to support all your kids, especially girl kids, to be self-reliant and strong, both mentally and physically. Thank you.

Satya's parents were overjoyed by their daughter's achievements. With his head held high and chest puffed with pride, Ramarao hugged his daughter. Rajeshwari brought sweets to feed Satya, but she put up her hand saying "keep them for brother", to her chagrin. Everyone laughed at that, but with remorse. Satya hugged her mother and took a sweet and broke it into two pieces to share with her brother.

14

BROKEN CHAIN

"What are you searching for"? asked Ramya, coming into the office room of Vishnu with a cup of coffee for him. "I kept my chain with the broken link here in this bowl where I drop all my coins. Today, I decided to go to the goldsmith, but can't find it now. Have you kept it anywhere safe?" asked Vishnu, taking the cup from her hands. "No, I have not even noticed. But how can it go missing? Except you and me, no one else comes to this room. Check again or may be, you have kept it in the bedroom cupboard. Let me go and check, said Ramya. "No, I am damn sure that I dropped it here when the link broke and the chain fell down. I was busy, so I didn't bother to go in again. After that, I completely forgot about it. Today, I was thinking about Avani Avattam(the day men change the sacred thread) and then remembered about the chain and decided to get it repaired as I am going out for the purchases. Are you sure no one else comes into this room? What about Parvathi?" asked Vishnu.

What about Parvathi? Yes, she does come to clean and sweep, but she is with us for more than 3 years now. And we never had any issue with her before, Ramya protested. "Let me go and check in the bedroom". So saying, she went inside. And Vishnu started checking his office desk and every nook and corner of the room.

After a futile search of the whole house for the next few hours, they had given up.

Just then Parvathi rang the bell and entered as usual for her daily chores. Vishnu decided to call and confront Parvathi about the chain in spite of resistance from Ramya, who kept saying, please don't, we don't have any evidence against her. So, how can we accuse her of it? But Vishnu was adamant and asked Parvathi point blank about the missing chain.

Parvathi was aghast. "Anna! How can you even think like that about me? I don't even ask for advance like others. I never expect anything, but my salary and am always happy with the new saree and bonus akka gives me for Diwali. Nothing more than that. Never had any complaint against me in the past 15 years. I am working in 3 other houses, if you want you can call and ask them about me". To and fro, the arguments continued and finally ended with Parvathi shouting "if you have any evidence, go and report to the police", walking out angrily and banging the door. Vishnu also left for the market, annoyed, but helpless and clueless.

Ramya heaved a sigh of relief and went and made herself a cup of coffee. While sipping her coffee, she called her friend and said "your plan worked perfectly Janu. I got rid of Parvathi who saw us together. To be frank, I don't think she ever had any plan of blackmailing us. But as you said it's better to be safe than sorry later. Who? Swamigal (sage) went to get his Poonal(sacred thread), she giggled uncontrollably! And now you know what? I also got a thick chain of at least 3 sovereigns in the bargain. With the price of gold skyrocketing, we can book for a nice retreat for the weekend, Vishnu is out of town on work. Okay now, let me go and look for another maid. Bye.

"Love you darling". Happily humming, she dialled the number of 'Maids for Hire'.

15

HARDENED HEART

The PVR theatre was full with patrons jostling with each other, hands full of popcorn tubs and soft drink cans. Rajat finally managed to reach the counter and grabbed a big popcorn tub and two coke cans. The movie, 'Murder without a motive' had already started, while he was stuck in the queue at the snack bar. Cursing his bad luck, he quickly opened the door marked Screen 5. With lot of difficulty, he managed not to stamp on the feet of people already sitting in their seats and reached his corner seat and slid into it, next to his fiancée Shoba. She was engrossed in the scene and didn't even turn her head towards him to acknowledge his sacrifice. Disappointed with this cold treatment, he nudged her a bit hard to take the coke can from his hand. Next minute, his terrified shriek filled the air, as Shoba just slid down from her seat and onto the ground in a heap.

The lights were on and people stood aside. The police cordoned off the area around the seats. The forensic team was busy trying to collect any evidence from the crime scene. People were so busy watching the mystery unfolding on the screen, that nobody noticed who got up and left after ten minutes into the movie. The body of Shoba was kept on the walkway where a doctor from the team trying to check for the telltale wounds on the body. Dr. Edith finally found a deep wound at the base of the skull. The initial findings suggested instant death due to a very sharp object which actually entered the stem of the brain. According to her, the murder weapon could be a ice pick or a thin knife blade. Finally, the forensic search team completed their work and the body was packed in a body bag and put into a waiting ambulance. A shocked and uncontrollable Rajat was given a sedative. The family members were also informed by police to come to the Government hospital for further formalities.

Suraj walked out of the theatre and into the busy road. It suddenly started drizzling as if it was sharing his grief. The tears flowing from his eyes were mingling with the raindrops. He stopped near a dustbin and after making sure nobody was watching, threw his hoodie into it and walked straight to the bus stop and got into a bus and finally reached tank bund and sat on a bench there. He looked at his hands and started weeping. How many dreams and plans for the future, all shattered in one stroke? His mind went back to his first year in the college. Coming from a small village in Telangana, he was very timid, but studious and industrious. He topped the college in the first year exams and Shoba had come to congratulate him. That was their first meeting. After that, it was Shoba who always came to him to clear her physics and chemistry doubts. He sincerely helped her by making notes and even did her lab reports.

Slowly, the friendship moved to the next level and turned into love. In helping her in her studies, he even neglected his own studies. Shoba always invited him for movies and picnics with her friends and it was his duty to get tickets for the first show and arrange the logistics for their outings. And whenever he felt that he was unsuitable for her, Shoba used to chide him saying look through my eyes and you will find your answer. He was so happy and proud that a beautiful girl like Shoba liked him for his looks and intelligence. His confidence and trust went for a toss when the other day he eavesdropped Shoba talking to her friends. How much she ridiculed him, saying "that stupid fool thinks I am in love with him! Can you imagine? Me, college beauty! Of course, I told him that he is my Mills n boon hero, tall, dark and handsome. And the best part, he really believed it!!

I befriended him just to get good marks without much effort. He typed all my internal assessments and prepared notes for all those important questions. I saved all the tuition money my father gave me. Not only that, we got a delivery boy cum bodyguard for free! Isn't it? Next month, my fiancé is coming back from US and it is also our finals. So, I will get rid of this dumbo on some pretext. The end". And laughter followed from her gang piercing his ears and heart. That day, he decided to take revenge on her for deceiving him and playing games with his emotions. His heart turned cold and hard into ice, devoid of all love and emotions.

Suraj kept his behaviour normal with Shoba. And finally one day, she confessed that her parents were pressurising her into marrying an NRI, but she is still trying to find a way out. She needed a little time to bring her family around, she pleaded. He didn't say anything and agreed to wait for her phone call. But he kept tabs on her and found out the day Shoba planned for a movie night with Rajat. He followed them and got a seat exactly behind her. He carried the ice pick, which ironically, Shoba gifted him on his birthday knowing his love for the Himalayas. The moment the lights went off, he quietly removed the ice pick which he taped to the inside leg of his jeans and plunged it into her neck when she was sitting straight, engrossed in the chase on the screen. She just slumped into her seat with a small whimper. He waited for a few seconds and slowly walked out of the theatre.

Suraj wiped his face as well as the thoughts of suicide from his mind. He threw the ice pick into the Hussain Sagar lake after wiping it clean with his hand kerchief. He will live with Shoba's memories for he sincerely and wholeheartedly loved her. But his parents sacrificed everything for him and were eagerly waiting for him to provide them with a better life. He has responsibilities of his siblings. He has to live for them, he decided. With a hardened heart, Suraj walked back towards his room.

16

DIVINITY

Rani, you come early tomorrow, ok? Don't give me any excuses after coming late. Last year, you came so late and everything got delayed", instructed Lakshmi again. "Got it Amma! How many times you repeat the same thing? Last year, I was sick but still came to work. Yet, you keep complaining about the same" retorted Rani.

Narayana, reading the newspaper, looked up and said "Lakshmi, my coffee, and let the poor girl go". Rani took to her heels immediately.

Lakshmi came with the steaming coffee cup and said "you don't understand. Tomorrow is Friday, Varalakshmi vratam and so many things to do! That's why I was reminding". ……. "But you have told her enough times. You get so worked up thinking about the vratam. How many times have I told you to keep it simple? No need of cooking 9 varieties for Varalakshmi. Make one naivedyam, keep some fruits and have puja in peace with good intention and concentration. God asks for Bhakti, not the number of sweets or savouries you have made. You spend more time in cooking than in praying on festive days. All these vratam and festivals are stipulated, so we keep our homes and hearts clean and pure", explained Narayana for the umpteenth time. But Lakshmi gave him a stern look and went back to the kitchen, grumbling, "no prayers, nothing for you. You always work or tinker with some broken down thing. That's all. If I complain, you come up with work is worship and such nonsense".

Little Lalitha was watching all this very inquisitively. She loved festivals and the rituals attached to them like making rangolis, floral decorations, visiting neighbourhood, etc. But the usual bickering between her parents, was always about the naivedyam. Dad wants it to be simple, so smma need not struggle in the kitchen alone as she insists on some special conditions like taking head bath and not touching others. And Rani too can't cut vegetables or scrape coconut for that day. Also, her grandmother was not supposed to help for some reason. When she asked why, no one answered. Later, her father told her that because grandpa is not there, she was not supposed to touch haldi, kumkum or prasad. Lalitha never understood the logic behind it. Why? What grandpa had to do with this? After all, he is with the God, isn't he? Then, why can't grandma prepare or do puja for Lakshmi? Why Rani can't touch amma ? Amma drops everything into her bowl but never offers her a plate like she does for others. So many questions in her small brain remained unanswered.

"Huh, finally done" said Lakshmi, counting all the 9 varieties she had made. She arranged all of them in a plate to offer as naivedyam(offering to the deity) later after the conclusion of the puja and sat down near the altar, where she had arranged the Varalakshmi and started her puja reciting the slokas with her mother-in-law sitting next to her. Puja was completed with all the rituals and finally came the part of offering naivedyam. Lakshmi got up and went into the kitchen to bring the plate she had arranged before she sat for the puja. But it was nowhere to be seen. She asked her mother-in-law and her husband. They too came into the kitchen and looked around, but the plate was not to be seen. Suddenly, Narayana heard somebody talking in the front yard and he went there, followed by his mother and Lakshmi.

Lalitha was sitting with the plate of naivedyam with a few kids in tattered clothes, happily eating the food from the plates in their hands. Lakshmi was aghast at that sight. Lalitha saw them and said "look nanamma(father's mother), Godess Varalakshmi came in the form of these girls. So only I took the plate of naivedyam to feed them. Remember you told me the story of Shiridi Sai, in which he came in the form of ants and beggar? See, I didn't shout at them. I recognised them when they asked me for food and served them. I did a good thing, didn't I?". Before Lakshmi could react, Narayana went and hugged Lalitha and said, "yes, dear, you did a wonderful job of feeding the hungry and needy. Go and take care of them. I am coming in a moment".

He then told Lakshmi", it's okay. You have more food in the vessels. Go and arrange another plate and offer it to the deity. But she is already very happy and blessed you, I bet. Annadaanam is the best daanam any person can do. God is always pleased by seva. So, now don't be angry at Lalitha but be happy that she is putting into practice what our scriptures and sages said, 'Serving humanity is serving divinity'.

That Shravan Varalakshmi remained a beautiful memory for Narayana.

17

NEST

"The nest is not only for laying eggs, it's a place where the chicks feel safe and taken care of, lovingly, by their parents. They were first hatched by the body-warmth of the mother/ father and later as small chicks, were fed by their parents. They were kept safe till they are adults and could manage their own life. Then, they fly away and build a nest of their own. That's how the cycle continues". The science lesson on birds by her teacher was imprinted on Mary's tender heart. At her home, everybody calls her 'devil'. Her granny everyday curses her saying, "devil, eaten her father even before the birth!". Mary's father died in an accident at his factory when her mother was pregnant with her. Though her mother Saramma never blamed Mary, she kept mum when others taunted her as they were dependent on their granny and Jacob uncle. She consoled her saying that "once I manage to get a job, we will live in our own house. Then, no one will blame you". So, Mary always dreamt of having a loving nest, her own safe haven.

Out of the blue, Saramma got remarried to John, the owner of the book store where uncle Jacob was working. He was a widower with twin boys aged 12. He wanted to marry and was looking for a suitable match, for a person who underwent a similar tragedy like him. Jacob felt it was a good opportunity to get into his boss's good books and also a great chance to get rid of his sister in-law and her kid. Everything went well and Saramma wedded John. John was a nice person and never interfered in anything. Though he loved Mary as a daughter he never had, the fear of his sons feeling threatened stopped him from showing his affection towards Mary. While Saramma, in her anxiety to make her second marriage a success, went overboard to show that her priority were the twins, she started neglecting Mary. She always cooked the favourite food of her husband and the twins. Christmas decorations and parties were according to the twins' preference. The twins never showed any interest in Mary, nor they bothered her. They were just aloof with Mary. With her mom busy with her husband and twins, Mary felt like she was in a stranger's house. She continued with her life and studies, but lost interest in everything. Mary felt alone in a house full of people and was depressed. Her studies suffered and she failed her 10th exam twice. Her only dream was to get married and have a nest of her own where everything will be to her liking and she will be safe and loved by the family. As Mary didn't show any interest in continuing her studies, John fixed her marriage with a distant relative from his side. George was good looking, well settled in business and the only son of widowed Theresa. The wedding was conducted with pomp and Mary was happy to move to her new home, her beloved nest, where everything will be to her choice and liking.

Mary entered her new home in Hyderabad with lot of aspirations and dreams. George was a good husband, but was busy with his business and he was devoted to his mom. After the initial euphoria of honeymoon, Mary found herself at home under Theresa's iron grip. Being a single mother, Theresa was very possessive about George. She decided everything at home and about George. Mary was not allowed any changes in the decor of the house, not even their bedroom. From George to kitchen, everything had to be according to Theresa's dictum. In her fear of losing control over her only child, Theresa became a dictator. Whenever Mary complained about it, George always consoled her saying, "It's only a matter of few years. As mom is old and not going to be there forever. After which this house will be all yours". Mary, as usual, adjusted and followed her mother in law's instructions. In a few months, she conceived and gave birth to a beautiful baby boy. He was named Thomas according to Theresa's wish. Even after that, nothing changed for Mary. Even Thomas was mostly with Theresa and she monopolised him. Only feeding him was Mary's job and he never really got attached to Mary. This was the last straw for Mary and she had a big showdown with Theresa. George tried to make peace between them, but failed. After that, friction and fights between them became a regular feature. Thomas grew up with all this unpleasantness around him, for which he blamed his mother. Theresa's old age and his initial attachment to her made him believe that Mary was to be blamed for all this. He moved away further from Mary. From baptism to his wedding, Thomas's life was decided by Theresa and Mary just remained a mute spectator in her own son's life.

Mary was unhappy and felt like an alien in her own house. In course of time, Theresa passed away and George retired from his business. Thomas became an engineer and started managing his father's business. He got married to Sara who was related to Theresa. Sara came home as a new bride to the house and took the reigns of the house on the first day itself. She was very sweet but firm and changed everything to her liking. Curtains, sofas, decorations, everything, and whenever Mary offered any advice, she made it very clear that it was her house and her choice. Mary was told, being an octogenarian, she could take recourse to the bible and spend time in prayers. Thomas was as usual, nonchalant. Though George understood Mary's pain, he watched helplessly to avoid further friction.

Mary kept thinking about her life and her dream of having a nest, like one, explained by her teacher. A nest, where she felt safe and loved. That's all she wanted, nothing more. With her heartache, she slowly became a recluse, eating and speaking very less. George tried his best to humour her, but failed in his attempts. One morning, they found Mary gone in her sleep peacefully. Atleast, death was gentle with her, thought George, remembering her struggle with life. Her father and even husband, though they loved her, never supported her nor showed it in action. Lived but never felt loved or accepted as a person. 'My poor Mary', grieved George.

Mary was taken in procession to the burial ground and after all the rituals, her body was lowered into the earth. The plaque on her grave read

Mary's Nest

1956 ———- 2019.

George and others placed bouquets on her grave and left her in peace.

18

FALL OF HUMANITY

"Ramya, pick up your phone, damn it. It's been ringing for the past few minutes and you are snoring as if someone is singing a lullaby", shouted a very irritated Arjun from his work table. Ramya pushed her hand out of the thick quilt and grabbed her mobile from the bedside table. Hello, she mumbled and then sat up with a shriek

"What are you saying ? Have you gone mad ? I spoke to him in the evening only. How's it possible?" Words were tumbling out of her mouth and tears were streaming down her cheeks. Arjun jumped and grabbed the phone from her shaking hands. He listened quietly for few minutes, then kept the phone down and pulled Ramya into a tight embrace. "Raghu committed suicide is what Rajen was saying. How and

why?? I am totally baffled". He gently rubbed her back and allowed her to cry, silently holding her and giving her the strength to absorb the shock.

Have some toast and coffee. We will leave after that for Niagara. I have checked the car and filled the gas, so we can go straight and reach within 2 hrs. I have already informed our offices, packed the bags and booked rooms in the hotel for our stay. Depending on the situation, we can change the bookings. Arjun had taken charge and Ramya was just following him numbly. Her mind was still not accepting the fact that her younger brother was no more. What was supposed to be a happy family union turned into an utter tragedy. She was cursing herself for not joining her brother and his friend on their trip to Niagara.

Raghu and his best friend came down from New York to Toronto during their break, as usual. They were just done with their final semester exams of Chemical Engineering from Columbia university. Four of them spent two days visiting the museums, art galleries and eating different cuisines. When they planned a overnight trip to Niagara, Ramya decided to stay back to catch up with her pending work that had accumulated over the past few days. She also thought she would utilise that time to prepare some home food, especially Raghu's favourite Pooran Poli and Kothimbir Vadi as a surprise. She even made some Carrot Kheer and prepared Idli batter for his friend, Rajender. She bought gifts and wrapped them. She was waiting excitedly for their arrival to have some fun with them and this sudden news of suicide completely shattered her.

After their parents' death in a car accident 10 years ago, the two siblings consoled and supported each other. Luckily, they had enough money from insurance and savings of their parents to pursue their dreams. After doing her masters, Ramya married and moved to Canada. Raghu joined a university in USA which was close to his sister's place and he kept visiting them regularly along with Rajender, whose family was back in India. She treated Rajender also just like her brother and always took care of his needs. Her mind was in turmoil throughout the journey, and she refused to stop even for coffee on the way. Finally, they reached the hospital and met a sobbing Rajender.

The police led them for the identification of the body. Ramya fainted after one look at her brother's body and was led outside by Rajender. Meanwhile, the Police officer gave all the details to Arjun . "Looks like a suicide by ingesting a chemical which left no traces in the body. After all, he is chemical engineer, wasn't he? No signs of any struggle or injury on the body, so we rule out any foul play. We are ready to handover the body after a few simple formalities. Sorry for your loss", he patted Arjun on his back and left to wait outside.

Rajinder started howling "I am feeling so horrible. I couldn't save my best friend from suicide. He was so cool and calm while saying good night. Never suspected he will do anything like this, just because Rashmi rejected his proposal. He said he is coming to terms with her rejection and will concentrate on his career instead. Never thought he will go to this extreme. We planned this trip just to start a new chapter in his life. Early morning, I went to his room to wake him up for our morning walk but he didn't answer the door, the intercom or his mobile. So, I got the staff open the room with the duplicate key only to find him dead on the bed. This Rashmi played with his emotions ....!

Wait, what are you saying ? Arjun got out of his stoop. "How do you know that Raghu committed suicide because Rashmi rejected him asked Arjun. We found this on his desk replied the sergeant and showed a letter placed in a clear plastic sheet. A letter addressed to Ramya.

Sorry Didi, I am unable to keep Rashmi out of my mind. She rejected my proposal after four years of courtship. Sorry, I kept you in the dark as you always told me not to get involved in any affairs till I finished my studies. You were right didi, I made a mistake. But now, I am unable to forget and move forward like her. I tried my best to be normal around you but it's killing me inside. She is my life and without her, there is nothing left in my life. Please forgive me Di.

Love you Di,

Good bye.

"No, no. Something is seriously wrong. Raghu is yet to propose to Rashmi, because he asked me how I proposed to Ramya and was asking me for some tips on it. He even wanted me to talk and convince Ramya to forgive him. He wanted Ramya's blessings before buying an engagement ring. This letter is a fake, planted by someone, who knows all about Raghu except the latest details. Sergeant this is not suicide. I strongly suspect this Rajender is behind his death" shouted Arjun and moved menacingly towards Rajender.

When Rajender was interrogated all things tumbled out. He was in love with Rashmi from the day he joined the university. But he never had the courage to approach her or talk to her. Meanwhile,

Raghu and Rashmi became close as both were from Mumbai and had lot of common friends and interests. So, he just cultivated friendship with Raghu and through him, with Rashmi. Raghu, who innocently considered him as his good friend confided everything about his promise to his sister and not disclosing about Rashmi to his sister, etc. So, finally when they planned a holiday in Toronto, Rajender also planned his revenge. Being a chemical student, he knew the properties of antifreeze which he started slipping in small doses in Raghu's food from last few days. Raghu neglected his flu like symptoms and just took some medicine to control it. After slipping the last lethal dose in Raghu's dinner at Niagara hotel, Rajender even typed a letter on Raghu's laptop and kept a print out, to make it look like a suicide. After making sure he removed all his finger prints, he went to his room and played his part next morning. His only mistake was not knowing that Raghu has already confided in Arjun about his love and Rashmi.

Ramya and Arjun returned home with heavy hearts but with some consolation that atleast Raghu's murder was avenged and Rajender was behind the bars. But with this episode, their faith over friendship, relationships and finally humanity, had taken a great fall.

19

THE NEW NORMAL

The Visakhapatnam airport was unusually crowded. Rajyam pushed her trolley through the crowds and noticed that many carried welcome placards and garlands. Oh, some dignitary is arriving, she mused and crossed the barricade and entered the airport lobby after completing the formalities at the gate. As she moved towards the luggage screening area, a smartly dressed police officer came and said good morning ma'am. Rajyam, taken aback for a moment, said good morning, any problem? I have all papers and .....no no ma'am, sorry if I scared you. But I am your old student Swapna, daughter of your close friend and neighbour Savitri. Remember? She bent down and touched her feet. It took a few minutes for Rajyam to recollect and react. "Yes, I remember now. More than fifteen years ! How is Savitri? enquired Rajyam. She is well, said Swapna and took her hand and guided her towards the VIP lounge and gestured the constable to take the trolley and finish the screening.

"Your flight to Chennai is delayed by one hour ma'am, so please come and relax here. Do you like to have some juice or coffee?" asked Swapna, with a wallet in her hand. Rajyam who was still in awe, blurted "are you the same timid girl who used to always hide behind your mother ? Shy to the core, never used to answer in the class without being forced? And now a police officer?? ".

Swapna laughed and said "yes, I am DSP, Visakhapatnam district. Today I am here to meet the central minister who is arriving from Delhi and by my good luck, I met my favourite teacher from school.

Yes, very true ma'am, like you said, I was very timid and shy in my younger days. But when we moved to Hyderabad, I faced many tragedies. Amma was due for her promotion, but had to resign due to harassment by her new boss who wanted some favours to give a favourable report. She went into depression and it took a lot of effort and time for the family to pull her out of that state. Then, my favourite cousin committed suicide as she couldn't face harassment for dowry and she was just 22 at the time of her death. All these left a very deep impression on my mind and I started writing poems, pouring out all my anger into them. When my political science lecturer, Mr. Sharma, saw my poetry, he praised me in the class and told all of us, the girl students to turn the anger we felt into something constructive. He said times are changing and we girls have to change. Don't wait for things to change but be the change. For the situation in the country to change, we need more women in all spheres of governance, he had said. Girls, only education is your weapon and knowledge is your power. Grab them". His continuous inspiration and guidance resulted in most of us giving UPSC and other competitive exams and I succeeded in landing in my favourite police service. Rajyam had tears in her eyes and wiping them, she said ", I am so proud to know that a teacher showed correct path to so many girls. Bless him. Yes , anger is also good when turned into positive energy. It propels you forward like a rocket. Yes, every girl should be a Saraswathi and Durga rolled into one. I am so happy to have met this new confident and inspiring Swapna. I am lucky to meet you my girl". She hugged her ward tightly and blessed her wholeheartedly.

20

A FRIEND INDEED

Lakshmi was busy making snacks for the evening tea when she sensed that Subha had entered the house. But she didn't hear the usual shout of "ma, I am home, what's for eating ?". She finished frying the remaining corn pakoras, arranged them on a plate along with tea cups on a tray and entered the dining area. As expected, Subha was seated on the chair but was looking very angry and upset. Lakshmi quietly placed the plate of pakoras and tea in front of her. They both had their tea in silence. Later, as usual, they walked out of the house towards the woods for their evening walk.

The oak wood park was close to their house and the evening walk in the woods had been a daily ritual for them for the past few years. That was how they shared everyday's events. But today, they walked in silence. After about ten minutes, Subha started " I am so angry with Fiona. The last six months, she was constantly wailing about Robert cheating on her and then, when confronted, how he dumped her for Angela. Had to sit through her crying sessions, consoling her, giving her undivided attention, keeping her humoured. I even invited other friends and made plans to keep her amused and busy. After all this, she now shamelessly says, Robert is back and had apologised for his foolishness and promised not leave her ever again . And she readily accepted his apologies. Can you believe it? No shame at all! He cheated her with her best friend and now she is ready to accept him back. I told her that if she is accepting Robert, then I am not going to be her friend. I can't be with someone who is so spineless and stupid". Lakshmi heard the whole ranting without saying anything.

They completed one circle and Lakshmi walked towards a bench and sat on it, pulling Subha next to her. She said, "let me tell you something similar which happened about ten years ago. One of my close friends' husband left her for his secretary. She took both her grown up kids and went back to her hometown. We were in touch and she shared her anger and anguish with me. I advised her to divorce her husband and demand a hefty alimony. I continued sharing her grief and eventually helped her in finding employment. Slowly, our correspondence decreased to one or two greeting cards a year. But after five years, I saw her posts on fb with her husband and children having a gala holiday time. Angrily, I called her and she confessed that her husband came back and apologised and now they are together. I got very upset and unfriended her on fb, deleted her number from my contacts on phone. But after a few years, I realised my mistake. I was angry because she didn't follow my advice of divorcing her husband. For me, the act of unfaithfulness is unpardonable. I can't accept such situation and can never forgive that person. But that's me. I expected my friend to be me. But she had chosen a different path for which she had her own reasons. Later, as l grew older, I understood that people are different and we react in different ways. This has a lot to do with the initial upbringing and later, how one evolves with education, interactions with people and the outer world. Some develop self-confidence, strong views, ideas and courage to live on their terms. Some choose to adjust, forgive and make compromises. It's their life and they have all the right to decide so.

As a friend, our duty is to help them in their need but we cannot and should not expect them to follow our advice as a binding. Let's not be judgmental. Live and let live should be our motto. Be happy and wish your friend good luck for her future".

Subha hugged her mom tight and said "what will I do without you? You always come up with a right answer in your storytelling way. Yes, I am being selfish and judgmental. Let me call Fiona immediately and apologise". Both mom and daughter sat there, while Subha called Fiona and had a wonderful chat.

21

DARK SECRET

"Dinner time", called Anitha playfully, banging the plate with a spoon. The table was already set and both Atul and Amar came out for dinner. As Amar stared at the items on the table, Anitha was getting ready for her lecture on the goodness of karela and lauki as both were disliked by him. But he took them quietly without any fuss and started his dinner to the dismay of Anitha. The conversation at the table was dominated by Atul who was excited about the latest App, he was working on and explaining the importance of it. Anitha, who was never interested in the tech-talk was busy thinking about her schedule for the next day!

Atul was still on his laptop, when Anitha eventually came to bed and slid into it. "Have you noticed Amar?" she asked Atul, who was busy checking his FB. "Why? What happened?", enquired Atul, with his eyes still glued to the screen. "He is being very quiet now a days. Didn't you notice? Today, I made karela fry and lauki curry as they were the only vegetables left in the fridge. He hates both the vegetables and I was expecting a war at the table. But he didn't utter a word and ate everything, chupchap. I was so surprised", added Anitha. "Mothers!! "groaned Atul, "he is growing up and adjusting. Be happy and proud. Instead, you were worried about that. May be, he is following my suit", guffawed Anil to Anitha's consternation.

He closed the laptop and kept it on the bedside table. He turned towards Anitha and said "you kept on saying he is being quiet, not fighting anymore and not demanding. Don't you realise he is now almost 13 yrs and showing maturity? That's all. Being a single child is not as bad as everyone thinks. Stop worrying and get some sleep. Tomorrow, you have an important meeting with clients, isn't it? So, relax and get some sleep. He switched off the light and in a minute, Anitha could hear his soft snores. Lucky guy, can sleep anytime, anywhere, muttered Anitha to self and tried to sleep, putting her worries on the back burner.

But Anitha's tension increased as Amar was increasingly becoming withdrawn, losing appetite and even losing weight. Even Atul noticed this and was alarmed a bit. Anitha checked with Amar's class teacher and other teachers. They also expressed their concern, but couldn't tell anything specific as to why, as nothing happened in the class room to trigger the change. He was doing his homework, but the enthusiasm was missing. They also commented that even Aditi was being the same and speculated a fight between them might be the cause for this change.

That reminded Anitha that the best buddy of Amar was not coming home anymore. Amar and Aditi were very close friends and she used to come home, almost every weekend, to study and play video games. They were inseparable even in school.

She returned home and casually asked Amar in the evening as to why Aditi was not coming home. His face lost colour and he mumbled something and went into his room and closed the door. This raised her suspicion and she decided to call Aditi's mother, but then decided against it. She didn't want to alarm Aditi's family with her suspicions.

That night, she saw a blue light flickering in Amar's room and went to find the laptop on and Amar fast asleep on the chair in front of it. She was about to close the laptop and her eyes fell on the screen and she stifled a cry. On the screen was the site to 'detergent and other household cleaning supplies for suicide'. She immediately ran out and called Atul to check it. They both looked at each other horrified and at the innocently sleeping Amar. Atul closed the laptop and they both sat in the hall, keeping a watch on him. Next morning, they both took leave from office and also told Amar to take a day off. After breakfast, Anitha and Atul sat next to Amar. Anitha said "we believe in you. Whatever happened or if you have done anything, we accept it wholeheartedly. But please talk to us. Share whatever dark secret you were trying to hide from us. Something or someone is bothering you and it's affecting you badly. We can see it and it's killing us. We can't stay silent any more. Do tell us. Whatever it is, we are with you. We love you, whatever it is. Just talk to us. Papa and I are always with you. Please, please beta" and she started crying. Amar also started crying and Started "mumma, it's not my fault. I didn't do anything wrong. But I am scared. I don't want to go to jail". Amar was crying and sobbing and started shivering uncontrollably. Atul held him close and hushed him. After sometime, Atul recovered and said " On Aditi's birthday, I gave her a card and a surprise gift during break in the school garden. She just hugged and kissed on my cheek to say thanks, like we always do. But Shankar, our school attender came to us and showed our picture which he clicked on his mobile and said he will make it viral by posting it on the internet. He said I will then be sent to jail because Aditi's parents will complain to the police or at least, I will be removed from this school and you will send me away to a hostel. I was very scared and Aditi started crying, saying her mom will kill her, if it happens. So, I begged him to delete the picture and he said he will but I have to do whatever he says. From that day, he calls me during break time and takes me secretly to his room behind the school and does all bad things with me. I hate it and it's also very hurting and painful. I beg him to leave me but he threatens, showing the picture. He says that he will reveal the secret to all. I can't eat or sleep. Papa, we didn't do anything wrong. But I am very scared. I want to die, but I don't know how". His pitiable cry mingled with Anitha's sobs.

Atul was shaking with anger and disgust. "How dare he? Scaring and blackmailing small kids for their innocent act. He thinks he can get away with that!!". He hugged Amar and said, "don't worry. You are innocent and that crooked fellow has done a very wrong thing. Now, you just relax and Papa will take care of everything". He told Anitha to take care of Amar and also keep close watch on him, as they were still shaken by the laptop incident.

Atul went and took the principal into confidence. They made sure that Shankar was in the school, when police in plain clothes came to arrest him. All of this happened in secrecy to avoid the media publicity to protect the innocent kids and also the school's reputation. The principal was aghast when he heard the news and was ashamed and very apologetic. He immediately took steps to place CCTV around the school for better security and also initiated counselling for all the students. He also made arrangements to check if any other student was also targeted by Shankar.

After a few months:

"'Ma, I hate this Palak !! I am not eating it", shouted Amar and it sounded like music to Anitha. "My boy is back ! Bhagwan, tera laakh, laakh shukar", Anitha prayed to her Ganesha and shouted back "nothing doing, Just finish it".

22

VINTAGE

Radhika looked into the mirror and groaned "huh, so many wrinkles and crow feet around the eyes. Even my face has spots all over". She tried using a concealer, three layers of makeup and shimmer to make it presentable, according to her standards. Her husband Pratap was patiently waiting in the hall, watching news on the TV and also checking mails on his phone. Two empty cups of coffee and a half bottle of water were there as a proof of his long wait! Finally, Radhika emerged out of their bedroom, still frowning into her compact mirror. She lifted her face and asked, Pratap. "how's my face? Better than morning? I kept chilled teabags on my eyes and rubbed ice cubes to reduce the puffiness around my face. Also, I did some facial exercises. Is my make-up fine? Is this dress too tight around my hips? She bombarded Pratap with questions like the rapid fire round in "Coffee with Karan"!

Pratap looked at her amusingly and said "Radhika, chill. Sanjay and his parents are coming to meet Sanjana. As you know, Sanjay and Sanjana were dating for the past five years and they decided to take the final plunge. It's just a formality for us parents to meet. And no one is going to judge you for your looks now. You are 65 and the bride's mother. So, relax". He offered her a glass of wine and then with a spark in his eyes, he added "to me, you are always beautiful dear. Your wrinkles show that you lived your life caring for your family. The crow feet and laugh lines are a proof that you had fun, laughed and enjoyed life. The lines on your tummy show that you carried and underwent all the hardships of pregnancy and endured labour pains. Your sagging breasts prove that you nurtured your children with love.

We all love you for what you are and how you nourished the family with your love, managed our day to day life, sacrificed your dreams and enriched our lives. For us, you are always beautiful in and out. Don't worry about your looks and about people's reaction. No need of hiding behind Botox or makeup. Be normal and let us face our age and grow with natural grace. For me, you are still intoxicating, "my old wine in the same old bottle"!!".

Radhika tried to look severe but her face relaxed and a small smile brightened her face. She lovingly looked at Pratap and said "you know how to talk. This smooth talk of you led me through the wedding altar and two caesareans! Let's cross this too. Thanks for all that praise and I expect some in action too, later in the night", she continued the banter and snuggled closer to him.

23

DAVID AND SAMBAR

Dar-es-Salaam, (Haven of peace) is the former capital, but now an important port city of Tanzania in East Africa. We moved there in 2007 and my daughters joined the Aga Khan School and I started my new innings to teach Economics to Diploma students in a local college.

As International school students, my daughters had friends from different races and religions. Africans, whites from different nations, Indians, Arabs, mixed race, you name it and we had them. Our house was pretty close to the school and my elder one who was doing her IB (International Baccalaureate) used to bring her friends home all the time. Everyone was welcome as we never had any issue with race, religion or gender. Only issue was when they start heated discussions and arguments, I used to feel 3rd world war will erupt then and there in the drawing room of our house and we will be held responsible.

The only rule in our house is /was, whoever comes, the food served will only be pure vegetarian. Even these kids were not allowed to bring in or order non-veg food.

So, they all not only got used to, but also started liking my veggie food. I always prepared food for them with very little spice, chillies to make sure they can handle our Indian food. As we know, nobody can handle our Indian spice and especially my hot Andhra food.

Hawa, a local Muslim lady, who was my house help then, used to literally cry whenever she saw me adding green chillies or chilli powder to my curries.

So, one day, I made my usual hot arachivuta sambar (typically Tamilian, made with freshly ground sambar spice) for a dinner party. As it was still hot, I left the bowl on the dining table, with instructions to Hawa to keep it inside the fridge later. I returned after my class and found the bowl empty. On enquiring, my daughter said that her friends came to study for some time and as David wanted to try sambar, She gave a small bowl to taste. But he liked it so much he finished the whole big bowl of sambar. She also added that he told me tell you that "he loved the lentil soup with veggies but wished there were few meatballs in it ". She apologised for the empty bowl and left.

I was aghast. Not for the sambar, but was scared and worried about David.

Of course, he was a huge 6 foot tall Tanzanian athletic boy, but they are not used to our chillies, tamarind and all the other stuff. I started sweating and swearing for leaving out my spicy sambar.

I don't remember anything or how I managed the party that night.

I only remember, that too very vividly, that I spent the whole night tossing and turning, worried to death about David. In one scenario, I saw him dead and police coming to arrest me for killing him with my deadly spice. In a second and better scenario, he was down with diarrhoea and doctors interrogating me as to what I fed him with. It was total nightmare. Just waited for the night to end.

Next morning, my daughter went to school and called me to inform that David was fine. Not only was he feeling fine, but wanted to taste Jaya's "Lentil soup again".

I went... nooooooooooooooo!

24

DESTINY

The bus stop was unusually quiet and Rama was sitting alone on the bench, lost in her thoughts. Today, she reached the bus stop very early and so had to wait for atleast another 20 minutes for her direct bus to the office. Rama was still trying to understand her mother's outburst. What was her fault if the groom's family had rejected her? That too, it was not for the first time. She had been rejected many times before and every time, the reasons were ofcourse, different. Sometimes it was about her skin colour, height or lack of it, her qualifications and the list was endless. But it was mainly due their financial situation and the absence of her father. Her father left them and married his colleague and sent divorce papers signed in black ink, blotting their lives with that ink forever. She could feel her mother's pain and disappointment, but why she blames me for that, was the cause of Rama's distress. Yesterday, in her anger amma, threw her notebook into the dustbin. The book which her favourite English teacher presented to her for getting 80% in her 12th exams. Kalyani ma'am encouraged her to write and read all her short stories. She continued that habit and wrote many stories, but never showed them to anyone else, as she bared her heart in those stories. Those stories reflected her thoughts about people and society, which blamed only her mother for the failed marriage, but had given a clean chit to her father. Any relationship depends on both the involved person's attitude and adjustment. Sometimes, it may not work inspite of all their efforts. Why blame only one person for it? Why live and let live, is not a norm of this society.........?

Rama's train of thoughts stopped abruptly with the blaring horn announcing the arrival of her bus. Rama got into the bus looking forward to the routine work to keep her busy and away from her gloomy thoughts.

"What a pleasant surprise my dear" the happy voice of Kalyani ma'am cheered Rama. It's very rare to hear from her teacher. Their calls were usually reserved for birthdays and teacher's day. So, she was surprised, but that phrase also confused her. "What's the matter ma'am?" asked Rama. "Just now read your story in the magazine, which you wrote a few years ago but never sent for publishing, in spite of my best efforts. Finally, you found the courage to follow your heart and dream. I am very happy for you and please continue with it. I am eagerly waiting for more stories in print from you. Stay happy". The call ended leaving Rama utterly bewildered. Her story published in that reputed magazine!! How? Who found her book? Her soul? Rama's head started throbbing with the unanswered questions. She took permission and left her office.

She took an auto and entered the office of 'The new woman' magazine'. Finally, she managed the postal address from which the story was posted. Thanking the editor, she left the office and wrote a letter to a stranger, introducing herself and asking how and from where he got the story. She gave her contact details and posted the letter, praying for a positive response.

A few days passed without any news and Rama lost hope of getting back her book of stories. One day, as she was stepping out of her office, she saw a stranger standing there with her office assistant Ranga. The moment he saw Rama, the stranger took a step towards her saying, "My name is Suresh". That was enough to bring a smile to Rama's face. After the pleasantries, they moved to a nearby coffee shop. Suresh gave her a gift bag containing her note book, one writing pad and an expensive pen. "I am so glad that I found your book and had an opportunity to read your wonderful stories. Your stories depict life and your beautiful thoughts on relationships, responsibilities of maintaining that relationship and everything. You should write many more such stories and publish them regularly. People loved your story as you can see form the mails. They were expecting more from you. Don't disappoint them. You should take up writing seriously. It was by luck I found the book thrown on to the footpath. Picked it up out of curiosity as the handwriting was so neat and I then read the stories. Except your name, no other clue to return the book. So, after much contemplation, I sent the story to the magazine in your name, hoping against hope that you or someone close to you will recognise the story and will try to contact me. In that hope only, I added my details. Thank God, my intuition worked and I found you or rather you found me" chuckled Suresh. Both left after exchanging phone numbers and promised to be in touch.

Rama became a celebrity within two years, with more than hundred stories published in different magazines and two books of her collection of short stories were also released. She left her job and was now a full time writer and regularly features on prime T.V shows. The friendship between the two friends was also blossoming, blooming and growing strong and deep.

25

UPBRINGING

Ramesh looked at the luxurious car parked in front of their small house. A uniformed driver was sitting in the car and checking his android phone. He glanced at Ramesh and went back to his phone with a bored look. Ramesh entered the house hesitantly, wondering who would have come to visit them in a chauffeur driven car.

A well dressed man and an elegant looking lady were sitting in plastic chairs, looking pretty uncomfortable in the middle class surroundings. The moment they saw Ramesh, they sprang to their feet and the lady shouting "my son, came and tried to hug Ramesh, who almost jumped to avoid it, shouting "what, who are you? This is my mom'.

He went and stood next to Lakshmi. "Noo, they are not your parents. They only raised you. In fact, I am your mother, who carried you for nine months".....before she could finish her sentence, "and left me on the steps of an orphanage and vanished looking for greener pastures, isn't it? added Ramesh. "Who told you all that rubbish? I had to leave you as there was no other choice for me. My parents didn't agree to my choice of life partner, so I was forced to leave you, but I have never forgotten you", sobbed the lady. "Really? After 20 years, you remembered me!! I am so fortunate", said Ramesh sarcastically.

The man then intervened and said "my name is Deepak and Rani is my wife and your biological mother. Due to unfortunate circumstances, she had to leave you and your biological father and marry me. We moved to Boston, as I have my businesses there. We were very successful, wealthy, famous and happy except for not having children. So, we decided to look for you and atlast, after five years, managed to trace you. As the address given by your parents at the orphanage was old and you people had shifted to a new city, it costed us, a lot of money and effort. But we succeeded finally, he smiled. But Ramesh didn't show any emotion and asked "but may I know why you were you trying to trace me"? Rani immediately stood up and said "so we can take you with us as our son and heir to our property. A life of luxury and a business empire is waiting just for you. Let's go. We can shop everything you need on our way to the hotel" gushed Rani.

"What made you think that I want to come with you? I am happy with my parents. They are always there for me. And am content with my life. Please leave", said Ramesh.

Krishna and Lakshmi were confused and speechless, watching all this drama unfold in front of their eyes. Lakshmi's heart was beating so fast and loud with anxiety and tension that she thought she was about to faint. The small, sick baby the father of Jesus and Mary Orphanage gave them for adoption changed their life completely. They named him Ramesh and it took many a month to nurse the sick baby to a healthy and happy child. They spent many sleepless nights to take care of him. And Krishna took up two jobs to manage the money for his medicines and special diet. All that hard work paid well. Ramesh never disappointed them. He did well in studies, sports, debates and all extra-curricular activities in school and now in college too. He managed to study well without any extra tuitions and bagged scholarships. He was a very affectionate and loving child, any parent would love to have.

Always very simple and down to earth, she can't see even a trace of it in his so called mother, Lakshmi thought sadly. Her mind became numb thinking about their life without Ramesh.

Krishna felt as if he was drowning into a bottomless pit. He was scared to even think of life without Ramesh. He was worried about Lakshmi's reaction. But then, he thought about the life awaiting Ramesh with his own mother and father. They should not come in the way of his progress. He looked at Lakshmi and she understood what he was thinking. With a heavy heart, she went to Ramesh and said "we both think you should go with your mother. After all, she has every right and it was destined because she managed to find you after all these years", trying to control her quivering voice and tears threatening to pour out of her eyes. Krishna stood with a stone face controlling his emotions.

A beaming Rani said, "even your parents want the same. Don't worry about them. I will pay them double the money that they have spent on you. If you want, I can even buy them a house as a parting gift from you. Let's go now. Today is a very auspicious day. So, let's not waste any more time. We should go and see the lawyer and discuss. So that in future, we won't have any trouble from these people".

Stop, shouted an angry Ramesh!

He then turned towards Deepak and Rani and said "you said you had spent a lot of money and time to find me. But my parents looked after me for 20 years. They took a month old sick baby into their arms and with their love and lot of hardship, nurtured it into a healthy and happy adult. You wanted a heir for your property, so you suddenly realised that you have an abandoned son somewhere and decided to pick him up. You were selfish. You jilted my biological father, abandoned me and went away happily. Life didn't teach you anything. You have not changed even an iota. Even now, you are the same selfish person trying to destroy somebody's happiness for your sake. You don't have any feelings for others. Sorry, but I can never forget you abandoning me, but can only forgive you, because of my mother's upbringing and the values nurtured by her. I belong to them and only them. And the luxurious life you are talking about, I prefer to earn on my own, with my intellect and hard work. That's what I learned from my parents.

Thanks for the visit, but you may leave now, Ramesh stood between Krishna and Lakshmi with his hands around their shoulders. Deepak and Rani walked out slowly, looking at their beaming faces filled with love for each other.

26

BLOCKBUSTER LIFE

"Nothing! I don't want to do anything with you. My lawyer had already filed a complaint against you. If you trespass again, I am going to call the police.

Just get out of my property and from my life forever" shouted Ramya and slammed the door on Anand's face.

She took deep breaths to control her anger and the shaking of her body. Slowly, her heart rate and breathing became normal. Ramya went inside and filled a glass of cold water and sat in her favourite spot in the hall from where she could see all her pictures on the central wall and the display shelf with all her awards and books. Her head rose high with pride and a feeling of accomplishment and contentment warmed her heart. She said a silent prayer for her guardian angel and her family. She slowly took a few sips of water and her mind wandered into her past.

Ramya was the youngest of the three siblings. Both her brothers, after college, got married and took over the family business. In spite of stiff resistance from her family, Ramya joined college to do her graduation in English. During her final year, their, whole class went to watch 'Othello' performed by an amateur drama company. The actors were introduced to the class after the play and Ramya promptly fell in love with the actor who played Othello. Initially, they exchanged looks, then smiles and finally phone numbers. This led to some long phone calls, then to meetings at parks and theatres. Finally, at the end of the year, they decided to tie the knot. As both the families were opposed to their marriage due to differences in caste and class, they quietly got married at the registrar's office with the help of friends.

The newlyweds set up their home in the outskirts of the city. Anand started as a sales representative and Ramya joined a school to teach English. Life was good and they were happy. Though the family boycotted them, they had their friends and colleagues. Two years went in a jiffy. Then, slowly, Ramya sensed some change in Anand's behaviour. Late comings and long and frequent tours became order of the day. And finally, he dropped the bomb shell and confessed that his parents were pressurising him to marry his niece as per their custom. He cannot refuse them anymore. He told Ramya not fear but she only needed to adjust to the situation and he will keep visiting her regularly. Horrified, Ramya packed her bags and went to her best friend and colleague, Sangita. She not only gave her shelter, but also the moral support and strength to Ramya. In due course, she applied for divorce and on mutual consent the marriage ended legally.

Ramya was completely shattered, but her family firmly closed the doors on her . It was Sangita who took care of Ramya like her own sister. She forced her to eat and gave her pep talk to pull her out of her gloom. Sangita's husband Rahul and her two kids showered her with love and treated her like family. Slowly, Ramya got a hold of herself and joined back school. She found a room close to Sangita and all her free time was spent with the kids. She loved playing with Raju and Riya and the best was the story time. As a kid, Ramya loved reading stories. And now, she started making up stories for kids with princes, princesses, demons, super heroes and their adventures which they enjoyed immensely. One day, just on a whim, she posted her story to a children's magazine. To her surprise, it was published immediately and the publisher asked her for few more stories for their upcoming book.

The book was received well and within no time, Ramya got busy with her writing. Her children novels won many awards and were also made into movies. Even her movies were blockbusters and got national and international awards. Ramya became a very popular writer and also made good money from royalties. She bought a small bungalow with all the amenities. But still, her weekly meetings with Sangita and family were the highlight of her busy life. Ramya became not only a well known author but also a social worker, for she never forgot her initial struggle and the support of Sangita and her family. With the money she made, Ramya started a women's shelter, where women were given training in different fields to empower them. She made Sangita and Rahul trustees for her NGO.

Her family tried to mend fences as soon as Ramya became famous and made money, but she kept them away. Anand tried in vain to prove his undeniable love and promised to leave his family forever. She was sick of his selfishness and shamelessness.

The sound of the doorbell brought her out of her thoughts and she hurried to open the door. Raju and Riya stood there with a big bouquet and Sangita, with a cake. Rahul started singing the happy birthday song and the rest joined him. Hugging them, Ramya silently thanked her Ganesha for giving such good friends as blessing,

I need nothing more than this Deva !!

27

A NEW DAWN

Endu chepalu amma, endu chepalu!!(dry fish), the voice of the seller was loud enough for Saraswatamma to stop chanting her Lalitha Sahasranamamam midway. She automatically covered her nose and gave choicest abuses to the fishmonger lady. "Everyday, my puja is disrupted by her shouts and the stink of that horrible fish! How many times I warned her not to shout", fumed Saraswatamma.

But attayya, she has to sell and here, except us in the colony, all eat fish and they want to buy in the morning. It's her business," her daughter-in-law Ramani tried reasoning with her.

"Bamma(grandma), actually God is testing your concentration and empathy. We are not getting any smell. It's only your imagination", teased Amala, her granddaughter.

'Cheepo, gaadida (get lost, you donkey)! Chinna pedda ledhu (no respect for elders)", shouted Saraswati. Ramani slapped Amala lightly on her cheek and glared at her. "Everyday, same drama amma, tell bamma to change her puja time instead", quipped Amala, as she left for her school.

Saraswati was born and brought up in an orthodox brahmin family and was also married into one. Her whole life was spent in a small village in Andhra where all these caste, creed, untouchability, etc still rule to the roost. She lost her husband early in life and along with her young son Prabhat, moved to stay with her brother in the same village. Luckily, she had enough land and fruit orchards, so never faced any financial problems. With the help of her brother, she sent her son to a good school and then to college. Prabhat,

"

though grew up in the same village, later moved to big cities for education which changed his ideas and perspective. He embraced new values and broadened his horizons. He settled well and married a girl of his choice. Ramani, his wife, was a freelance designer and photographer. They moved around the country during his tenure with a public sector bank. Amala is his only daughter, now studying 9th standard.

Prabhat recently joined as a senior executive in a corporate bank in Visakhapatnam . and brought Saraswatamma to stay with him and enjoy her old age in comfort. She was loving the big house with a garden near the beach and basking in the love and affection of her daughter-in-law and grand daughter. But she was not happy with the servant maid earlier, whose caste was not known as Prabhat strictly warned her not to indulge in such talk and now with this fish lady. Coming from an agraharam (Brahmin locality), she found it repulsive that fish, meat, etc were sold near her house. In her village, they were sold in a different market, not mixing up like here. She fumed, thinking about the supermarket she recently visited with the family. Rama Rama, same shop selling vegetables, fruits, meat and fish !! Kalikalam, kalikalam !! (Final Yuga and the end of human race), Saraswatamma banged her head with her palm in anguish.

The next morning, Amala and Prabhat left for school and office as usual.

Ramani kept everything ready for Saraswatamma on the table and left to attend a business meeting. Saraswatamma, after her breakfast, wandered into the garden and was looking at the roses, when suddenly, felt a jolting pain in her left arm and gave out a cry. She felt a little giddy, took a few steps and just collapsed. Finally, when she opened her eyes later, she found herself on a hospital bed with a tube in her hand. Ramani, who was sitting near her on a chair, immediately called the nurse, and moved closer and asked "how are you feeling now? Thank God! Great disaster averted!". The Doctor and nurse came and did the check-up. She was advised medication and a few more days of hospital stay.

After a couple of days, Sarawatama was back home and relaxing on her bed. Amala was giving her medicines when she asked her "what happened that day? I only remember the pain and then, the darkness. Nobody was at home that day, so, how did I reach the hospital? Whenever I ask your amma and nanna (mom n dad) about it, they are evading the topic. You tell me". Promise me not to get angry, said Amala and when her grandma nodded her head, she continued. "That day, as usual, the fish lady was on her way back home, when she saw you give a shout and fall down. So, she came rushing in, called and saw no one at home. She shouted for help and got our neighbours to call for an ambulance and shifted you to the hospital immediately.

The neighbours then informed dad and then we all came rushing. She was with you in the ambulance, holding your hand. Luckily, she got you within the golden hour to the hospital. As you suffered a massive heart attack, anything could have happened, the doctors said. When we came to the hospital, she was sitting outside the ICU praying for you. Only after the doctors declared you were out of danger, she left for her home". Saraswatamma was speechless and slowly, tears trickled down from her eyes. Amala got scared and was about to shout for her mom, when she heard a familiar voice talking to Ramani. Sarawatamma too recognised the voice and asked Amala to bring her in. Amala ran out and came back with the fish lady and a worried looking Ramani. Saraswatamma, with folded hands thanked and apologised to Satyavati, the fish lady. A very embarrassed and nervous Satyavati enquired about her health, chatted for a few minutes and took her leave.

"Lo, look at them. I wonder what these two have in common", mused Amala, looking at Saraswatamma and Satyavati, who were sitting in the verandah and were in deep conversation. Now, it's common to see Satyavi entering the house, (of course leaving her fish basket out) and sitting on the verandah to chat with Saraswatamma who even saves some Prasadam(holy offering) for Satyavati.

'A new dawn for both', said Ramani, looking at them happily.

28

SERIAL KILLER

"Jalaja", called Satish loudly from inside the bathroom. What? Shouted an irritated Jalaja who was engrossed in a Telugu serial on TV. "No water in the toilet. Did you on the pump this morning"? Only then did Jalaja remember that she didn't switch on the pump. "Oh, sorry. I was about to, but then, that suicide and in that tension, I forgot," replied Jalaja. Satish came out of the bathroom and anxiously asked "who committed suicide?" I will know only in the next episode. That was in the 'Sandhyaragam' serial, replied Jalaja. Satish gave her one angry look and went into the bedroom to change into his pyjamas as anyway there was no water to bathe.

He sat at the table for dinner, but no sight or smell of food. The table was empty, except for the plates and glasses. "Jalaja please, let's have dinner a bit early. I missed lunch due to some urgent meetings. Had only a sandwich and coffee". There was no reply, but he heard Jalaja calling up Pizza Hut and ordering pizza for dinner. "What, pizza again? This week, this is the third time we are eating pizza, "grumbled Satish.

"What can I do? As the provisions were over, I planned to go shopping in the morning but then this suicide and I got so upset not knowing what's happening. Luckily, my friends called and we all went to the mall to control our tension. After some shopping and lunch with friends, I felt a little better and came home and slept. You men don't understand how stressful it is to watch and wait for these episodes. For you, your meetings and deadlines are simple routines. But for us, daily a minimum of six serials to watch and remember all the characters and anticipate the next move is very difficult and nerve wracking!! Have you ever given a thought about me? You never watch or talk about any serial, always office and sports. You are hungry and that's why I ordered pizza as it is delivered fast. So, let's have some wine and pizza and go to bed early. Tomorrow, I have to see whether I am right or Sangita. We both had a bet of Rs.1000 on the outcome of the suicide".

Jalaja finished her talk to see a dumbfounded Satish with his mouth agape!

29

PAYING GUEST

Happy birthday to you, sang all the elders of the Prasanthi old age home. Harsha, after blowing out all six candles on his jungle themed cake, took the fancy knife to cut it and offered a piece each to his parents. Rashmi and Rajesh, after feeding him some cake, got busy in cutting the cake and arranging it on plates for distribution. They also arranged for a sumptuous meal for all the seniors of the home, taking their age into consideration. Rashmi being a doctor, made sure that all items were prepared hygienically, healthy, easily digestible and also tasty to the palate. Warm rotis, mixed vegetable curry, cutlets, kichdi, kadi, curd rice and kheer, with their appetising flavour filled the air and tantalised the taste buds of all the elders.

All were seated around tables and began their lunch. Rajesh and Rashmi were going around supervising. Suddenly, Rajesh stopped and looked at the couple and said in dismay "Braganza aunty, uncle, how come you are here?. The couple looked at him in confusion. Rajesh bent and touched their feet and said "I am Rajesh, your paying or rather non-paying guest at your home during my college days. My mother Savitri also visited and stayed with me. Remember? Slowly, a look of recognition came on to their face. Oh, after so many years. That cute one is your kid! aunt Elizabeth gushed happily. But uncle Philip was quite and looked very uncomfortable to meet in such condition. Rajesh called Rashmi and introduced her to them. Rashmi greeted them warmly and said "he always talks about you, Anthony and Mary. Please do have your lunch and then we can talk in leisure". She led her bewildered husband to the other side and said "I know you are quite upset to see them here. But don't make it so obvious and make them uncomfortable. We will talk to them later leisurely. Now, just be normal and take care of the lunch". Rajesh nodded his head and stepped into the garden.

Rajesh was still unable to stomach the fact that his beloved aunt and uncle are in a home, inspite of having two well educated children, for whose betterment, they struggled everyday. He saw their sacrifices for the sake of their children. How they both worked 24*7 to educate both of them. They ran a paying guest accommodation in Colaba, next to their bakery. They converted their ancestral home into a paying guest accommodation, which housed almost fifty paying guests working in different

fields. All guests were taken care of like a family by the Braganzas. They were served fresh bread rolls, scones, cookies and various types of cakes fresh from their bakery along with elaichi chai for breakfast and at tea time. It was in this accommodation that he stayed during his struggling days looking for a job. After his father's untimely death, he completed his engineering with scholarship and landed in Mumbai looking for a job. He stayed with the Braganzas for almost a year. His mother worked as a school teacher and supported him financially during that time. But the money orders used to be erratic and many times, there was a shortage of money. Aunty and uncle not only allowed him to stay without rent, but also fed him food free of cost during that difficult period. "We are in the same boat son. We understand how difficult it's for your mother. Don't worry, when you get a job repay with interest, okay? During that time, he got affected by typhoid and his mother Savitri came to Mumbai to take care of him. She stayed with him for two weeks and the couple provided all the required monetary and emotional support to her. His mother was so grateful and happy that her son was under their care and shelter.

During his stay, Braganza's son Anthony was doing his final year engineering and his sister was doing her internship after medicine.

Both were busy and he never had much interaction with them. Luckily, after his struggles for more than a year, he got a good job in Sydney and moved there. He sent his first salary to Braganza's with his mother's consent to show his gratitude. He kept in touch with them for few years and received Christmas cards from them. But then suddenly the letters stopped and his letters were undelivered as the addressee was not found. He came to India after a 5 year stint in Sydney and got married to Rashmi. He went to the Braganza house and bakery but it was sold and no one knew the whereabouts of them. But he and his mother never forgot them. Savitri always prayed for their family's welfare at every mandir she went and lighted candles in every church she visited with her son's family. Even on her death bed, she remembered and spoke about them. They left such a great impression on her.

He came out of his thoughts with Harsh pulling his hand calling out aloud, Baba! Rajesh smiled and swooped him into his arms and carried him and went into the hall.

Next day, both Rashmi and Rajesh came to the home to meet the Braganzas.

Uncle Philip was tight lipped, but aunt Elizabeth spilled the beans. On Children's insistence they sold their ancestral home and bakery for a handsome price and gave it to them. Anthony promised that the new apartment will be registered in Philip's name and they are going to live together. Mary took the remaining money to build a hospital and she promised to pay them monthly for their expenses. But after one year Anthony moved to England and sold the house discreetly. When the new owner came to evict them, Philip realised that he was deceived by his own son. Mary also pleaded helplessness as she was not yet settled and dropped them at the old age home. Now, she was married and living luxuriously, but not bothered about them.

Philip, who was always proud of his children's achievements and stood by them

inspite of all his difficulties was severely hurt and it can be seen in his eyes and drooped shoulders. He was looking much aged than his 68 years. Compared to him, Elizabeth was looking better though bitterly disappointed with her kids. Rajesh and Rashmi took leave after sometime, promising to come again.

After a month Rajesh, Rashmi and Harsh came and announced their decision to take them home. Rajesh said "we need grandparents for Harsh. My parents are no more and Rashmi's parents are in America with her brothers, who were settled there. Her parents are too old to travel, so we only meet them once in two years when we go to visit them. Harsh misses having grandparents around and your presence will fulfil that and for us having elders at home to emulate good values". When Philip was about to object, Rajesh handed him an envelope containing papers for Braganza bakery. He said I know you don't like charity, so I bought this bakery which was up for sale. You both can manage the bakery with your loyal staff who are eagerly waiting for your return. As you told me you can pay me back with interest. Come and stay with us. We need each other to make our family complete. Harsh came and took Philip's hands and said "We even arranged your room and dad said you both are going to bake yummy cakes and tell me bed time stories. Come, I can't wait anymore!"

Philip's face slowly creased into a broad smile and that brought a warm glow to Elizabeth's face.

"God bless my children", she hugged both Rashmi n Rajesh with a happy smile.

They moved with happy smiles and firm confident steps, clasping each other's hand into their future.

30

DREAMS OF WINGS

"Good morning, time for run". Shankar's wake-up call sounded like death knell to Chandra, who was cosily sleeping under the fluffy duvet. But as she knew there was no escape, she got up and went to the toilet to get ready for a gruelling schedule. She had to finish her run, gym routine before her school time. Getting ready and attending school, then again the same exercise routine after school for 2 hours. No holidays or excuses from this routine. No parties or outings with her friends. No junk food. Strict maintenance of weight. She gritted her teeth and hid her tears and strived to achieve her father's dream.

After a hot shower and dinner, with sleepy eyes and tired body, she completed her homework and studies, before hitting the bed dead tired. Inspite of not studying for enough hours, Chandra managed good grades and was always in the top five from her class. But Shankar was never impressed with her academics as he wanted her to fulfil his dream of becoming the no.1 gymnast of the country.

Shankar worked hard during his youth to make a name in the field of gymnastics. But he never went beyond the district competitions. So, finally, he left his quest for the gold medal and continued his studies and ended up as a government gazetted officer.

He married Kausalya and prayed for a son to fulfil his dream. But when he was blessed with a daughter, he felt dejected. But later, he decided to concentrate and make her into a number one gymnast. So, from the age of six, he started coaching his daughter to fulfil his dream. But Chandra hated it as her dream was to become an aeronautical engineer. Whenever she looked up to see the sky, her dream took wings and she got lost in her dream world. But she never had the courage to express her feelings and dreams as from her childhood, her father was talking only about his dream and it became very clear to her that it was the sole purpose of her life. Her mother never had any opinion or voice in that matter. So, Chandra was resigned to her fate and continued the training and won at the district and State level competitions and was now preparing for the Nationals.

Shankar felt humiliated with Chandra's performance at Nationals. She lost badly on vault and beam routine. Her jump from vault was so bad that Shankar walked out of the stadium in anger. Both returned home by afternoon flight. Shankar was silent from the time the competition ended. Chandra was feeling miserable and was crying throughout the journey. Both didn't touch even a morsel from the previous day. After reaching home, Shankar went straight to his room and slammed the door. Kausalya took one look at Chandra and hugged her tight and took her inside. After a hot shower, Chandra went into the hall and heard Shankar's angry words "she wasted all my time and energy. I spent all my money and this is what I got in return. All these days, I boasted about her and I will now be humiliated by all". He kept on ranting and then suddenly, Kausalya's voice rang out aloud, "why are you blaming Chandra? Was it her dream? Did we ever bother to ask her about her dream? What she wants to do?" Then suddenly, she started sobbing and said, "yesterday I was cleaning her room and suddenly a book fell from the book shelf. I was about to put it back and then saw all those pictures of aircrafts, spaceships, rockets, etc. And some notes and list of colleagues and universities. We never treated her like a child but treated her as a puppet to fulfill your dream. I failed as a mother miserably. I have fallen in my own eyes. I am ashamed to look into her eyes". Chandra ran and hugged her mother. Kausalya wiped her tears and said "now you work to achieve your dream. Our dreams cannot be yours and it's not your duty to compensate your father". A dazed Shankar too came and hugged and the three of them walked towards a new dream.

31

SUNDARA KANDA(BEAUTIFUL CHAPTER)

Revathi woke up with a start as she heard the bathroom mirror rattling. Later, she felt her steel cot sliding, furniture moving and crashing. She ran out of her room into the hall, screaming "get up, get up, all of you. Amma, Baba, Dadi, wake up. Earthquake, move, move". Her mother, father, grandmother, all of them woke up immediately, though still a bit groggy. Her brother Ramesh also came running out of his room and they all moved out of their old, dilapidated house. In just a few minutes the walls came crashing down, throwing out rubble and dust swirled up in circles, making it difficult to see or breath. Revathi and Ramesh, between them, managed to shift the elders to safety, into an open space. The few minutes of fury of mother earth was sufficient to destroy their life!

Their house was gone, and with it, the furniture, Revathi's valuable books, Ramesh's secondhand laptop, all shredded and shattered. Whatever were their meagre savings, all gone, as the sudden crash brought the roof down and nothing could be salvaged. In a few seconds, they lost their house, money and had become homeless urchins. Earth's rambling's gone in few seconds, devastating the whole village. No building was left standing. Trees were uprooted, electric poles snapped and wires were left hanging and sparks flew dangerously.

Wiping her face of dust mingled with hot tears, Revathi looked around to see the utter devastation all around. People were pouring out of their houses, which were swaying precariously! All around it was only rubble and dust swirling in circles and fires burning.

The dust and heat were unbearable and everywhere, people were running, calling out the names of their beloved ones. Howling, crying and cursing the Mother Earth for turning into a murderer of her own offspring. Revathi's mother Sumati, a teacher in a primary school, was sobbing uncontrollably looking at the shambles of the school building. Her father, Shankar, a retired head master, was stunned and speechless. Only her grandmother Sitadevi was thanking her favourite Lord Hanuman for saving their lives and keeping them alive and together. She touched Revathi's shoulder and gestured towards the Sitarama mandir, which was miraculously still standing intact, except for the broken boundary wall and a few uprooted trees. They all moved towards the temple, with Sumathi still sobbing and cursing all the Gods for the devastation. Sitadevi tried consoling her, but to no avail.

Sitadevi's father was a priest in the local Sri Sitarama temple and from him, she had learnt to recite Ramayan. She loved reciting it, especially the chapter of Sundara Kanda, which is all about Hanuman and his adventures, his unlimited powers, and his unfaltering faith in Rama. It had become her lifelong companion. She recited it everyday without fail, only after which she partook her first morsel of food for the day. Even to this day, at the age of ninety five, she is hale and hearty. Not only she does all her work, but also helps Sumati in her daily routine. She never raises her voice, but always listens to others' problems and gives solutions. She led her brood calmly to the temple chanting Hanuman chalisa. Ramesh, an agnostic, was seething with rage. The future looked bleak and dark thoughts were crossing his mind. How he wished that the house collapsed and buried all of them under it's debris! For once, all their problems would have been solved. He tiredly traced his feet towards temple, lost in his cynical thoughts. Shankar was just holding on to his mother's hand and following her, just like in his childhood, drawing strength from her and feeling secure. Revathi was holding Sumati close to her and followed her grandmother, amazed at her calm demeanour, in spite of the chaos around them.

The temple was seething with refugees from all the nearby villages. The Government and a few NGO's swung into action and arranged for some food, water and other basic facilities. Combing operations were carried out and a few people were rescued alive from the debris and sent to the nearby city for medical treatment. Few unfortunate bodies were recovered and the last rites were conducted. The emotions in the camps were running rampant. Some were happy to find their kith and kin, while some were sad as they lost their loved ones. The only person beyond all these was Sitadevi. Reciting Sundara Kanda, she went around, hugging and consoling people in distress, offering a prayer for the departed soul. Congratulating the family and thanking the God for the miracle, she was one tireless soul offering her shoulder to one and all, providing the much needed love, warmth and moral support to the shattered people around her. Her faith in her lord was as great as Hanuman, she believed that whatever happens is for good, but Ramesh couldn't see anything good in their situation. He was slowly slipping into depression. His sudden bouts of anger and the subsequent silence got everyone worried about him. Revathi tried pulling him to do some volunteer work alongwith her, but failed. She continued volunteering her time to the NGO and was helping them in various capacities. During her work, she also interacted with Ajay, a young and handsome volunteer, who was brilliantly helping both the NGO and the Government workers. He took charge of everything around and in a short time, managed to provide temporary shelters to the affected families with all basic facilities like common kitchen and dining, medical, toilets and even a temporary school to keep the children occupied. Revathi was helping in organising everything and so was Ajay. In between all the chaotic activities, love blossomed between them and was steadily nurtured by both. To Revathi's relief, Ajay succeeded in getting Ramesh to work with a contractor who was given a tender to erect a multi-storey complex for the quake victims who lost their homes. He was now busy with the work and recovered from his depression. Shankar too joined an NGO and found a purpose for his life. Sumati started taking classes in the makeshift school and was happy.

The inauguration of the new housing colony was simple and the houses were allotted to all the victims by the handsome, ever smiling, young collector, who was none other than Ajay. He came as a volunteer to avoid all publicity and to get things done without any bureaucratic problems. He announced his engagement to Revathi, to the cheering crowd. Meanwhile, Ramesh got a permanent job with the contractor and shifted to a new house allotted to them, along with his parents and grandmother.

In a couple of weeks, the wedding of Ajay and Revathi took place in the community hall of the new building, without much pomp but with the affectionate crowd showering their blessings wholeheartedly on the young couple. Even the earth smiled as new plants sprung up with flowers galore.

In all this, the only person who never lost faith in God and in his actions was Sitadevi, who stood reciting Sundara Kanda during the wedding, seeking blessings for newlyweds in their Sundara Kanda of life.

32

DIARY

Arpita came home in a very bad mood, went straight to her room and slammed the door. Sumati and Ratna looked at each other and Sumati could sense that Ratna didn't approve this behaviour of her daughter and was about to go in and start a lecture on manners!! She understands her worry, but being the grandmother and a buddy of Arpita, she cautioned Ratna to be quite and leave Arpita alone in her room for sometime to calm herself. Ratna took her mother in law's advice and went into the garden to control her anger.

After about half a hour, Sumati knocked on Arpita's room, quietly, calling her chinna, may I come in? On hearing a feeble yes, she entered the room. Arpita was sprawled on the bed with her eyes and nose red and swollen. Her face was still wet with tears and the cheeks were smeared with mascara. Sumati sat next to her, took a napkin and wiped her face clean. She offered some water from the bottle on the bedside table. Arpita sat up and took the glass from her granny's hand and had a few sips of water, trying to control her hiccups. Sumati sat rubbing her back in silence, without asking any questions or giving any advice. This quality of Sumati was admired by all in the family. She always comforts people, without prying or judging them. She is a buddy and a confidante of Arpita, who shares all her secrets and problems without any fear of rebuke. Today was no exception. Arpita slowly started her story. "I told you na, that I like this boy, Srikanth, in my school. I really really like him and even Sakshi knows it. As it is, Srikanth is popular, being the school sports captain and a merit student. He being my senior, I am trying to get his attention by playing badminton, which he plays regularly and also joined the drama club. Luckily, he spoke to me a few times in the drama club and I was hoping that we will become friends very soon. But now, Sakshi also joined the club and is trying to woo him with her knowledge of dramatics. Today, she took him to the canteen to discuss about the upcoming play, but she didn't invite me. She is supposed to help me in befriending him, but looks like she is competing with me!".

Sumati controlled her smile. Okay, best friends vying for the attention of their first crush! History repeats itself, she thought and her mind went back to her schooldays. Nanamma!(granny in Telugu), Arpita's call brought her out of her reverie, "Wait for a moment. I have something for you, Very interesting, in which you will find something similar to this. I will get it for you. But you go first, have a wash, change and eat something. When you are hungry, your brain doesn't work. As it is, now a days it's not working, thanks to this Srikanth", she winked at her grand daughter. Arpita laughed and got up from the bed, curious about what granny was going to show her.

After the wash and some warm noodles in her tummy, Arpita went looking for her granny. She found her in her room, going through a note book, chuckling to herself. She jumped onto the bed and looked at the notebooks covered with brown paper, labelled 'My personal diary' and the years written on them. Sumati took one of them, checked the year and then gave it to Arpita saying, "my diary, which I wrote when I was in the ninth grade, just like you". Arpita was amazed and asked "you wrote diary? And you are giving it me to read. Really?". For which Sumati answered with a smile "no secrets between buddies". Then she added "I read the book 'Diary of Anne Frank' which inspired me to start a diary. I wrote diary regularly when I was in school and I wrote about everything in detail. But I didn't have proper diaries, so I made note books into diaries by covering them with paper and putting some stickers. During my college, I wrote a diary but not in a regular diary". She laughed at her own joke and said "okay, now you read what I went through when I was of your age. Ok? Let me go and finish my evening walk in the garden, I will be back in 40 minutes". She packed all other notebooks into a box and then kept them in the wardrobe, locked and left, leaving Arpita with her diary/notebook.

Sumati remembered her school days and her best friend Jyotsna. Both were neighbours and also classmates. Used to be together all their waking hours.

Both were good students and participated in all the events in school. A new boy, Ankit, joined the school. His father was an officer in Railways. He being from Bombay, was very sophisticated and well dressed, compared to the boys of the small town, Visakhapatnam. His hairstyle and mannerisms were like that of the popular hero Devanand. Both were smitten by him and that created a rift between the two good friends. They competed with each other to attract him. Both tried copying makeup from movie magazines, taking yummy food from home for him. The competition became so severe, that they stopped talking to each other. Their concentration on studies suffered and both ended up with poor marks in their half yearly examinations. Even their parents noticed the change in their behaviour and the growing distance between them. But when they were asked, both came up with some stories. Their teachers and classmates, everyone noticed it, but no one recognised the point of conflict. This went on for almost the whole year. Both tried to get close to Ankit and become his girl friend, just like they show in the movies. But poor Ankit, never had any idea of this rivalry or competition. In spite of his fashion and sophistication, he was a simple boy and wanted to make friendship with both the girls, who were popular for their academics and extracurricular activities. He never suspected anything and was happily enjoying all the attention. Meanwhile, due to some family issues his father took a transfer to his native and Ankit left saying goodbye to both his friends. He took their address and promised to keep in touch, raising their hopes for another type of romance, love letters etc. But sadly, the exchange of letters stopped within a few weeks as Ankit got busy with the new school and friends.

Sumati and Jyotsna both suffered in silence. They realised their folly and in a few months they rekindled their friendship and were back together, just like before. From that day to now, recalled Sumati fondly, as she took her mobile to send a message to Jyotsna who was visiting her daughter in London.

She finished her walk and went back to see Arpita in deep thought. She looked up and said "Nanamma, is it the same Jyotsna, your friend ?? "and when Sumati said "yes", she countered "but you called her Rakshasi (demon), Deyyam(monster) and some other names in your diary". Sumati laughed and said, "Yes, just like you I was angry and vented out all that in my diary. See, after all that misunderstanding, we were able to come together and be friends to this day, because we were very close and had good understanding. Actually, that rivalry taught us the importance of good friends. Because after Ankit left, we both realised that we were not happy while fighting for Ankit and missed each other very much. It was just that momentary selfishness which blinded us. After that, we vowed that we will never allow any third person to ruin our friendship. Having a good friend is a blessing and never lose it for stupid reasons. Tomorrow you talk to Sakshi and you both try to be friends with Srikanth. Then only you will realise what exactly you feel about Srikanth. Having a healthy friendship is the first step to any other relationship. In friendship, let there be no rivalry. Okay? reasoned Sumati. Arpita came and hugged her and said "thanks for allowing me to read your personal diary. It helped me to understand, that I was feeling jealous of Sakshi and after all it may not affect my friendship with Srikanth. Thank you for always being there. I will also try and build good friendships like you, 'the forever kind!"

Sumati hugged her back and Ratna, who came looking for them, joined them saying, 'group hug'.

33

LESSON FROM PUPIL

Prabhat entered the class 12 and immediately there was pin drop silence. Students were scared of their Chemistry teacher Prabhat. He was very knowledgeable and good with his subject, but very angry and impatient. He insults and humiliates the students so much that everyone in the class hates him wholeheartedly. He threw the paper bundle he was carrying on to the table and thundered at the students, "get ready to receive your marks". He barked each name and marks and the ones who got less marks got their papers and abuses thrown at them.

Everyone knew about their teacher's bad temper and braced for it, but it was still difficult to bear the brunt. The last name was Raghav's who was a very good student but this time didn't do that well in the test. And Prabhat was so angry that instead of the paper, he threw the duster at him, which struck Raghav squarely on the jaw. Raghav howled with pain and started bleeding from the gums. He was hurriedly escorted to the school's first aid room and was given treatment. Later, he was called to the Principal's room for enquiry. Prabhat was standing there with ashen face, looking nervous. When the principal asked about the teacher throwing duster at him, Raghav assured the principal that it was only the paper which was thrown at him and that he had gingivitis, as a result of which, sometimes his gums do bleed. He thanked the principal for his concern and time and went back to his class, leaving a stunned Prabhat standing there.

Raghav reached home and followed his daily routine. After his tea, a few rounds of shuttle with his siblings, he studied for a few hours and had his dinner. Around 8 PM he packed his bag and went to the nearby library, where already a few elders were sitting in a circle with slates and chalks ready. Raghav took out from his bag a few text books, notebooks, pencils and erasers, to the surprise of the gathered elders and distributed them to all. Then, he arranged the blackboard on the wall and started his class. He wrote a few sentences and then went around to see and correct the mistakes of his students. Patiently, he went to each one and helped them in writing and recognising the letters. When a few stumbled, he sat next to them, held their hand and made them trace with a lovely encouraging smile on his face.

One of his students, Shankar held his hand and said "how can we ever repay you beta? You came to our slum and encouraged us to take up studies instead of wasting time on drinking and gambling. You are teaching us how to read and write, calculate, use mobiles for our business and also hygiene and general awareness. You are spending your time and pocket money on us. We can only bless with our whole heart" to which everybody nodded their heads with moist eyes. A very emotional Raghav replied "I am not doing anything for free. You are not aware of the satisfaction and happiness I earn by teaching you all. The feeling that I am doing something worthy is giving me so much confidence to lead my life well.

My teachers at school are my idols. Compared to them, I am nothing".

"You are much better than most of us Raghav", suddenly he heard the voice of his teacher Prabhat. He got up quickly and went to greet him with folded hands. "I came to your house to apologise and was told about your evening classes and so I came here to see", saying that, Prabhat held Raghav by his shoulders and said "today, I learnt a valuable lesson from you. It's not how knowledgeable you are, but how much you are able to impart is important. You are happy sharing whatever you have acquired, that too for free and with lot of affection and patience. I am ashamed of my arrogance, impatience and ill treatment meted out to my students. Today, my pupil by saving my grace, taught me a lesson in humility and forgiveness. Your passion for teaching and patience will definitely make you a great teacher and I am so fortunate that you are my student. Hereafter, you will see a new Prabhat, I promise! "So saying, he hugged and blessed Rahgav and the quite night reverberated with happy and enthusiastic clapping of Raghav's pupils .

34

SEASONS OF LIFE

The Sun was playing peek a boo with many dark clouds swirling in the sky. The trees were looking fresh with the green leaves shining after the light showers in the night. Radha finished her one hour brisk morning walk and was now walking slowly, admiring the beauty in her surroundings and inhaling deeply, the earthly smell mingled with the fragrance of flowers scattered on the mud road. The fragrance of petrichor always brought a smile to her face. Few simple things she enjoyed in her life like getting wet in the rain, enjoying the fragrance of the earth and a strong cup of filter coffee. 'All is well', she laughed out aloud and opened the gate and entered her house. She slowly removed her shoes and wiped the mud from her shoes with a rag and kept them in the shoe rack in the porch. She shook the wet newspaper thrown on to the porch and spread it on the small table to dry and tiptoed in.

Her parents were still in bed sleeping cozily in the cool weather with light blankets pulled up to their necks. In the next room, Roja, her younger sister was fast asleep. While Radha was the obedient daughter, Roja was a rebel star.

Radha quietly went into the kitchen and spooned some coffee powder into the filter, added water and switched on the filter. She then took out milk from the fridge and " kept it for boiling. She got her application forms and pen and sat at the dining table going through them, while waiting for the milk to boil and the coffee decoction to be ready. Soon, the fresh brewed coffee fragrance enveloped the whole kitchen. With two mugs of strong coffee and a few Marie biscuits by her side, Radha was almost through her applications, when Raghava Rao entered the kitchen looking for his morning's elixir and instead, he found something very bitter. One look at Radha sitting with the application forms spoilt his mood and he shouted "won't you allow us to live in peace ? Is this necessary now? We had endured enough disgrace and mud slinging because of you. Atleast, think about your younger sister. Just stay at home and let us live in peace. Enough of tamasha. Not anymore"!!!! His thunderous voice brought Roja and Satyavati running to the kitchen.

Radha gathered her forms and left the kitchen quietly, leaving the other three standing there. Roja was the first to recover and retorted "you don't have to worry about me naannagaru (father in Telugu). With akka's life, I too learnt my lesson. Will never allow anyone to decide about my life.

Why you blame akka(sister) for your mistakes? Just because she is timid and silent, you blame her for your failure"........."How dare you?", screamed Raghav Rao, but before he could slap her, Satyavati held his hand. Raghavrao glared at both of them and stormed out of the house in a rage.

Radha sat looking at the garden out of the window. Her mind was in turmoil and went back to her childhood, her grandparent's village, where she was called Krishna's pellam (wife) from the day she was born. Krishna was five years elder to her and was her father's nephew. Lakshmi was Raghav Rao's only sibling and they had a very close bonding. Raghav Rao doted on his sister and never allowed anyone to come between them. He also showed great respect and affection towards his brother-in-law. So, when Radha was born, it was decided that she will be Krishna's wife, which is a very common alliance among Telugus. They always met during summer holidays at their paternal grandfather's house, played together and were good friends. After their schooling, Krishna opted for science and went to study in Hyderabad and then to IIT Kharagpur. And with time and passing away of their grandparents and with Krishna's busy schedules, they seldom met. Radha too got busy with her graduation but were in touch through an occasional letter. After his graduation, Krishna left for his higher studies in US.

Suddenly, one day, they got the news that Krishna decided to marry a classmate of his in the university. Though his parents were initially upset, they later gave in, respecting his decision. But Raghav Rao took it as an insult. He was deeply hurt by his sister and brother-in-law who expressed their inability to force Krishna to marry Radha. She pleaded with her brother saying "what's the use in a forced marriage? Nobody will be happy. Let's look for a better alliance for Radha. She is my responsibility." But Raghav Rao was filled with anger and resentment. His love and trust for Lakshmi took a severe beating and he broke all his bonds with his sister and decided that he will get her daughter a foreign groom just to get even with his nephew. Within three months, he fixed Radha's marriage with a business executive in Chicago through a marriage bureau. In spite of many objections raised by Satyavati and Roja, he went ahead with the marriage. Radha was overwhelmed with the turn events, kept silent and agreed to the marriage.

Shankar was very polite and reserved. During the marriage and afterwards also he hardly spoke to Radha, but even she being a shy person, nobody gave a thought.

After the wedding, he immediately flew back to Chicago as he came to India just to get married on a short vacation. He said he will apply for Radha's visa after submitting the marriage certificate and other proofs. After her wedding, Radha went and stayed with her in-laws in Hyderabad for three months and then returned home to Vijayawada. Even after six months, no news about visa, not even a single phone call or any communication from Shankar. Even his parents were evasive in their replies. Finally, after lot of coaxing from Satyavati, Radha tried calling Shankar, but failed. Ragahav Rao decided to go and confront his parents and that day Radha received a letter from Shankar, in which he confessed that he married only due to coercion and it has no future. His parents were aware of his partner John, but were not willing to accept it publicly. Just to save their reputation in the society, which is yet to accept the sexual orientation of a person, he married Radha. He confessed his guilt and betrayal and apologised. He enclosed a divorce notice and the papers and begged Radha to sign and end the marriage on mutual consent. He also agreed to pay alimony and implored her to accept it and start life afresh.

Raghavrao was devastated. From a simple happy go lucky father, he turned into a stone faced man filled with loath and hatred. His nephew's betrayal, sister's rejection of his love and affection dented his heart and Radha's failed marriage and the divorce completely shattered it.

Two letters changed the course of her life and Radha lost all interest in her life. She suffered from bouts of anxiety and depression, which led to eating and sleeping disorders. Her body and brain, both went out of control. Roja took responsibility and took her to the psychiatrist for regular sessions. Though younger to her by a few years, she stood up to their father when he objected to that. She took her to parks for walks, yoga and meditation class. Got her good books to read and sat with her, watching movies. Slowly, Radha picked up the shattered pieces and her life limped back to normalcy. Satyavati was with her in her struggle and nursed her lovingly and patiently. Radha completed her postgraduation online with their help. Since the past few months, she had independently started going out on her walks and other classes. She was now trying to apply for a job and that caused a lot of friction with her father.

Her failed marriage and subsequent divorce caused a lot of humiliation to the whole family. As no one knew the real reason for the divorce, there was a lot of speculation with sly remarks. Even her character was questioned and the family's name was dragged through mud. But in all this, what was my fault? pondered Radha. I was obedient and did whatever my father wanted me to do. It didn't work out and my life was ruined. But instead of showing some love and sympathy, why does he blame me? Radha was caught up in her deep revere and a gentle hand on her shoulder brought her back to the present. Satyavati came and sat next to her and held her hands.

"Your father shouts to cover his guilt. To pamper his ego and on rebound, he got you married and it's hurting him like hell that he ruined your life. Please forgive him".

Radha hugged her and said "I have not forgotten anything amma. How much fun we used to have and how supportive he was. We were such a happy family, reading and watching movies together, outings with friends and playing antakshari. He always gave us freedom to choose and do whatever we wanted to. But life made him a bitter man and this guilt is making it worse. More than I, he needs a psychiatrist's help. We can't just leave him like that anymore as the mental toll will affect him physically too. We need to help and support him, like you and Roja supported me. I am not the only one who suffered this ordeal. Naanna suffered more than I. Now it's time for us to unite and talk to him and seek some help before it's too late. I was immersed in my own sorrow and grief and failed to see how much naanna suffered through all these years. Let us promise ourselves that we will face this together and emerge as a happy family that we were before. Together, we can do". Roja came in and hugged and said, "I am in. I am an expert in psychology now. Let me corner and tackle Mr. Rao". And all of them erupted in laughter and after a long time, the house heard such hearty laughs. The roses and hibiscus in the garden also heard the laughter and swayed in the wind happily.

"Let's celebrate the occasion with a brunch. I am ordering on swiggy. No cooking, nothing. Good food, coffee and some antakshari is what we all need now. Go and get ready. I am calling Hotel Sangeetha to place the order and also naanna to apologise and call him back. Goo" ordered Roja.

Radha went for her bath and Roja heard her singing "Aaj phir jeene ki tamannah hai" and left with a smile on her face.

35

WHEN THERE IS A WILL

Gobbiyyalo gobbiyyalo...!

Sankranthi pandugavacche gobbiyyalo........(Festival of Sankranthi has arrived.)

(During the month of December, round balls made of cow dung, decorated with turmeric, kumkum and flowers called gobbemmalu, are placed in colourful rangoli and young girls go around singing gobbi songs, invoking goddess Gauri which is a tradition of Andhra.)

Young girls from the Alankar Society were singing and dancing around the gobbemmalu and Shashi came running, holding her silk parikini(full skirt) and singing the song loudly. Immediately, all of them stopped singing and closed their ears, saying "shhhhh...Abba!! Shashi paadake(please,don't sing)! How many times we have to request you? Your voice is so gruff. You just join us in clapping and dancing, no singing please", chimed Sarasa, the gang leader. Shashi, though felt hurt, covered it up by smiling and joined the group to dance around the gobbillu silently.

Shashi was 13 years old and loved singing. Her dream was to become a great singer like M.S. Subbulakshmi whose songs were played over and over at her home. Her mother, Ramani, was a Carnatic classical singer and a teacher. Her father, Ramesh, though an Engineer by profession, loved music and was a trained singer too. Both wanted their daughter also to be a great singer, but unfortunately her voice was very gruff and grating, not at all suitable for singing. And she didn't like any instrument like violin, veena. etc. She was adamant that when her parents just sang without help of any external instrument, why should she carry one around? Even she wanted to be like them, free to sing wherever and whenever she wanted. Her parents couldn't convince her and left it to the almighty Goddess Saraswati to give her some wisdom.

One day, while looking for some rare songs, Ramani suddenly came across a Youtube video of Elapata Sivaprasad. She shouted with joy,"Shashi, Shashi come fast! Look what I found. Exactly the medium you wanted". That night, all three of them sat and researched about the whistle wizard from Bapatla. Finally, that night after a long time, Shashi slept happily and peacefully.

The stage was set and the auditorium was filled with patrons eagerly waiting for a rare musical feat, that too by a female! The program was inaugurated by the lighting of the Diya by the Chief Guest, a well known music critic. It was followed by a few speeches for some more time, by which the audience got bored and started booing and clapping loud. The organisers, understanding the mood of the people, completed the formalities quickly and announced the main program of the day.

"Carnatic musical concert by Padmasri awardee, Miss Shashi, accompanied on violin by Shri Jayaraman, on Mridangam by Shri Venumadhav, and on Ghatam by Pt. Vinayakaram". Shashi came on to the stage and took her seat in the centre of the musicians, resplendent in a bright orange Kanjivaram saree with a purple border, a big bright orange bindi and a long thick plait with a big jasmine strand, Shashi was beauty personified. After greeting the audience with folded hands, she started her concert by invoking Vighnaharta Vinayaka. There was pin drop silence in the auditorium as everyone sat mesmerised, as she skilfully whistled the Dikshitar Kriti 'Vatapi Ganapatim' in Hamsadhawani ragam. Carnatic music through whistle, that too by a lady in full traditional attire. People had only witnessed whistling during movie scenes or rowdy acts on street. This was completely new for them. The audience sat still through the two hour concert and erupted in thundering applause at the end of it and gave Shashi a standing ovation.

Ramani and Ramesh looked at each other with content and silently sent a prayer to Ma Saraswati for fulfilling their daughter's dream.

36

NEW HORIZONS

Ramarao came home and shouted excitedly, "Saru, where are you? I have a good news to share! Saru!".

"Hold your horses, I am coming. Let me finish chopping these greens", replied Sarasa from the kitchen. "Damn your greens! I came with such a wonderful news and all you care about is your keerai!" bellowed Ramarao. Sarasa came out of the kitchen, wiping her hands with her saree" Arre Baba! Sorry, now tell me", she pulled a stool and sat down smiling. "What's the good news?"

Ramarao said with a beaming face "our Kamala was liked by that boy from Nashik!

Actually, their whole family liked her on the day, we met each other formally for the bride seeing ceremony. Even their horoscopes matched perfectly, said his father".

Sarasa exclaimed "What, really? Yedukondalavada, Venkatesa!" She immediately stood up and went to the prayer room to thank her favourite God, the Lord of Seven Hills, Tirupati Balaji.

"Our Kamala is really lucky. She is stepping into a rich and cultured family. Well educated boy with huge family business and property, but still very humble and simple. No show off, whatsoever! Simple and down to earth people, raved Sarasa.

Kamala came in with a heavy load of fruits and vegetables and dropped the bag onto the kitchen table. She went to wash her face and arms and came back wiping her face with the towel and shouted "Amma, lemon juice. It's so hot outside. I almost got roasted in the sun in that vegetable market. Hot and sweaty", she said, with a tired face.

"No more sun and getting roasted. Here after, you will travel only in air-conditioned cars and there will be no need to go to these stuffy markets. You can go to malls to do your shopping", enthused Sarasa.

Why? We won a jackpot? wondered Kamala. "No, stupid. That boy, Anand from Nashik liked you. Not only that, horoscopes too matched. You are going to marry soon and become Rani of Nashik" said Sarasa happily.

"Nooo! I don't want to marry that boy" shouted Kamala, shocking her parents.

"What did you say? You don't want to marry that boy? Have you gone mad?

Any girl will give her right arm to be in your place and you are refusing it?

Highly educated boy, good family, family business, everything and you say you are not interested? Why? Are you in love with someone? Hiding it from us?" thundered Ramarao.

"Nothing of that sort! I don't want to live in Nashik. I checked the other day on google. No big shopping malls, no fashion street, no good restaurants, no pubs. Nothing to enjoy life. What will I do there? All my married friends are living in Bangalore, Mumbai, New York and me in Nashik? I too want to be in big cities and do all those I read in magazines", declared Kamala. "Also, I have my boutique here which is now growing well with many regular customers. I have many plans regarding the future of my business. I can't jeopardise them now by moving to a God forsaken place", she concluded in a firm tone, giving no scope for any argument. She took her lemonade and walked to her room and closed the door firmly and also the conversation.

Ramarao and Sarasa were aghast at Kamala's decision but were unable to convince her for the wedding. Ramarao picked up the phone and apologised for the turn of events and was very much relieved and happy, when Anand, instead of getting angry, wanted to try and convince Kamala.

Kamala was surprised to see Anand at her boutique, but invited him warmly, like any of her customers. He asked many questions regarding the quality of clothes, designing and about the materials and their procurement. Kamala too patiently answered all his questions, secretly wondering about the mystery behind his appearance.

Anand said "I did my masters majoring in viticulture and oenology from a top university in UK" and when he saw her raised eyebrows in confusion, he laughed and said "viticulture is all about growing and harvesting grapes outdoors while oenology is the process of wine making from grapes indoors. My family was in this business for generations and it was only with the wisdom and experience passed down from generations of their workers. Just like vines, which firmly root in the ground, but grow all over in all directions by taking support from whatever is available around them, I too wanted to grow far and wide. So, I went to pursue the knowledge and was back to my roots, to strengthen them. When I met you at that art exhibition, I saw the same passion for knowledge and firmly rooted behaviour in you and admired you. My admiration for you grew into love, without my slight knowledge. It started spreading like a vine all over my heart.

I convinced my father to arrange a meeting between the families to know each other better. Alas! my mission failed miserably, smiled Anand sheepishly. Kamala was speechless at the turn of events and just stared at him.

Anand went on to say "yes, Nashik is a small place but you can always start there and allow the city to taste new fashions and be a trendsetter! I love travelling and reading, you also enjoy the same hobbies. We can work hard in our respective fields for six months and the remaining time, can tour, tasting and imbibing new fashions and trends, in both clothes and wine. We can spread our business to different countries but with our roots firmly in our motherland".

"No hurry, take your time to think and decide" so saying Anand walked out, after paying for the few items he picked up from her boutique. Kamala stood there thinking!

"Wow! This ice wine is really fabulous! Actually I am loving all these wines and the Niagra! Canada, you are beautiful" raved Kamala and then looking at his amused face, shouted excitedly, "love you Anand! Your love completely engulfed me like a vine. Long live vines and wines!!".

37

♡

MIRROR MIRROR ON THE WALL

"Here is your beeeggg bundle of joy". Smiling at her own joke, the nurse, handed over me to my mom at the maternity hospital. And that joke stuck to me like a permanent label, na, tattoo for life.

Myself, Latha even at 34, still struggling with that label of big girl/ fatty/ fatso.

When I was in school, I auditioned for the role of princess in the 'Snow White and

wicked Queen' play. I rendered all my dialogues well with gusto but the teacher insisted that a fat girl can never be a princess and instead of a princess, offered me the role of a tree in the forest. All the other participants laughed when he said that and I ran out of the auditorium to escape from their nasty comments. But it left a deep scar on my psyche and after that, I never ventured into dramatics though I was good and loved being an actress.

In college, no one called me Latha and an adjective was always added. It was either fatty or fatso. Some even called me Tuntun! Naturally, I never had many friends, but only a few, who understood and stood by me during my adolescence. Not only friends, my relatives made fun of me. Whenever we met for dinners or parties, some tried offering me more food saying, "eat however much you want, don't worry! There is plenty". Some came up with suggestions on dieting, workouts etc, making me hate those functions and also the people.

The problem here was, I neither had any health issue nor I suffered from anything. In spite of eating less and workouts, my weight remained the same. I was born big and remained big in spite of my best efforts. I tried intermittent fasting, Ducan diet, GM diet, but nothing worked. Joined gym and worked out for hours, still of no use. Finally, my family doctor warned me against all those diets and advised me to eat healthy, do regular exercise, be happy and ignore others.

Thank God, my parents stood by me like a rock and supported me against all odds.

Otherwise I would have been broken completely by this societal norms of normal size.

My escape from all these was academics. I immersed myself in books and more books. I read class books, classics and fiction, whatever I could lay my hands on.

My thirst for knowledge was never ending and I completed my Ph.D by the age of 26 and started working as an assistant professor in the university. But I could still feel the same humiliating looks from my colleagues and students, which made me wonder if education and knowledge do not make a difference, what will? Why society has this belief that everything should be according to their standard? Size, shape, dress, sexual orientation, all in set standard without deviation?? My head was filled with these questions with no escape from these thoughts. Finally, I found my answer in Victor.

Victor joined our university as an overseas visiting professor from Canada. His mother was from Tanzania, a Muslim and father was from Philippines, a Christian. Both met as students at the university and got married after a long courtship of 4 years. Victor was 7 years old when his dad died in a car accident. His mother, unable to bear the grief, moved back to Tanzania, hoping for parental and clan support. But they were not willing to accept Victor as one of them due to his fair skin and facial features, which he inherited from his father. He was ridiculed and was constantly harassed by his cousins and schoolmates. Without friends and in the new environment, Victor felt stifled. His grandparents never accepted him and he was outlawed. His mother too was helpless as she tried to fit into their rigid society. Though financially independent, she needed their support to settle back with her kin. She gave into the parental pressure and remarried. But after a few years and the birth of twins, her husband deserted her and married another woman.

Everyone blamed her for the failed marriage. All this trauma pushed her into drugs and she spent all her earnings on them, leaving her children to their fate. Victor, from the age of ten, became the bread winner and took care of his half siblings without any bias. He did part time jobs and continued his studies and with the help of some philanthropists, completed his graduation and found employment. Later, with his savings, he moved to Canada being a natural citizen and later, brought his family as his mother also had citizenship. He made sure that his siblings got good education and helped his mother to overcome her addiction. His patience and wisdom finally brought his family out of doom and they prospered well.

After narrating his story, he asked me "did you really face so much of humiliation or hatred? Did you face any racial oppression? Financial crisis? Did you face racial discrimination? Was unaccepted by the family or faced any financial crisis?

If no to all these, then why are you still stuck with that one word, "fatty" for life?

Few nasty comments from your peers and relatives robbed you of your confidence!

People look for an opportunity to poke fun or humiliate. Don't allow them to make you feel helpless. What is that so called society but a group of people like us?

You need not preach others but follow your path with confidence and see many will follow you. You stand up and let others do the same. Together, we can change the thought process of people and allow the norm of unity in diversity. We are all made up of different sizes, colours and shapes. We think differently, but finally, we are all humans with feelings. One day, when we will realise that, the world will be a better place to live!

Stop acting victim and stand up. Be bold and face the world squarely and then see! Why someone's words affect you so much that you try to escape into your cocoon? Why somebody's words matter so much that you stop meeting your friends?"

Victor's words made me realise the truth I am running away from. Yes, I was and am a coward. In spite of all my comforts, love and affection of parents, education and financial security, I am still waiting for society's approval for my physical appearance.

With that self-realisation, I stepped out with a spring in my stride. I wore what I wanted and attended my classes with a bold smile and new confidence and saw my detractors taking a step back as I marched on in my life.

"I love myself for what I am! I don't need anyone's approval or validation",

I told my reflection in the mirror, with a huge smile on my lips.

38

BELIEF

The sun was just climbing into his chariot and the clouds were welcoming him, floating around. Swathi was sweeping the front yard while surveying the road with her sweeping glances. Finally, she noticed Karan standing behind the shrubs and her face brightened with a smile but she continued with her work, as if she has not noticed him. She swept the yard, washed, and then proceeded to draw patterns with rice flour. She finished her floral pattern and took time to survey it from all angles, making sure that her face was visible to Karan in the most flattering manner. Then, she moved to the front garden with a silver basket to collect flowers. All the time she was walking around the plants, she kept smiling and throwing fleeting glances at Karan, who stood transfixed to the spot looking at her with a big smile on his face. Both were unaware of their surroundings, drunk on their puppy love.

All this was being observed by Nagaratnamma, from her vintage point on the terrace. She had come to dry her saree and then stood there silently watching the drama. 'What a shame', she thought 'the handsome, well behaved and intelligent boy doesn't belong to our caste! Otherwise, she would have tied this alliance. But now it's not possible, they belong to a different caste and have to follow the customs. Though she loved Swathi, more than anything in the world, she couldn't bring herself to commit such a crime'. After her parents' death in an accident, Swathi was brought up by Nagaratnamma. She took great care and made sure that she studied well along with the usual skills like cooking, stitching, singing etc

etc and provided for all her fancies. But this was beyond her. With a heavy heart, she decided that she had to put an end to this before it goes too far. She already heard through her trusted lieutenants that on the way to college and on bus some exchange of letters had happened. She came down the steps and called Swathi who immediately came running. Nagaratnamma's heart missed a beat looking at her radiant smiling face and felt sad remembering the task ahead of her.

In few weeks, Swathi found herself married off into an affluent business family from Guntur. The boy was well educated, good looking and managing the family business. Both his brothers were married and blessed with two kids each. Being the youngest bride, Swathi was pampered by all. Her husband Rajesh was very loving and cheerful and really took care of her whenever she missed her granny. Slowly, Swathi adjusted to her new life and forgot all about her past. Between taking care of family and helping kids in their work, three years went off in a jiffy. Slowly, the family and friends started asking, initially as a joke, but then with some concern, about starting a family. Even her in-laws started enquiring. Finally, Nagaratnamma took initiative and arranged for Swathi's check up. The doctor did all the tests and to their relief, confirmed that all is well with Swathi and now Rajesh need to undergo a few tests to detect the cause. After some hesitation, finally, the news was given to her in-laws and Rajesh. As expected, they did not like the idea of Rajesh proving his manhood !

With a lot of reluctance, their in-laws agreed to it, but they insisted on consulting only a doctor of their choice. After few weeks, they were told that the doctor has given a clean chit to Rajesh and thus started the blame game. "Our other two sons had kids and as it is, nothing wrong with our family. If at all there is a problem, then it is with your girl only," declared Swathi's mother-in-law.

Nagaratnamma tactfully eased the situation and suggested to take Swathi home to get her checked up properly and also try some native medicines. Being a shrewd person, Nagaratnamma understood that now Swathi's in-laws were never going to accept that Rajesh needs medication or allow any other modern methods to get a child. They will only blame Swathi for it and she has to bear their grudge. For the first time in her life, Nagaratnamma cursed the patriarchal society for it's bias and the way it treated women. After reaching their home, Swathi confessed about the snide remarks made by her sisters-in-law and mother-in-law. She even confirmed that her in-laws were thinking of remarriage of Rajesh, to prove that the problem lies only with her. This made Nagaratnamma very anxious and she started looking for a solution. And suddenly, she had a brilliant idea. But Nagaratnamma knows the difficulty in the execution and more over, she had to convince Swathi, another hurdle in the path. She went to bed thinking about it.

The next morning, she sat oiling Swathi's hair. She kept rubbing the aromatic oil into her long tresses and started talking about her college days and friends. Updating Swathi on who got married to whom in the village and outside, their kids and other gossip. She casually mentioned Karan and his wife, who is now at her parental house for her second delivery. Swathi's back stiffened hearing Karan's name from her granny's mouth. She wondered how did she know about Karan. Nagaratnamma slowly said" I am sorry dear. I did know that you both liked each other but never had the courage to tell your families. But I was scared to go against our society and it's rules and regulations. So, I arranged for your marriage at the earliest. But unfortunately, now the problem of fertility is rocking your marriage. Your husband will never go against his family. He is both emotionally and monetarily dependent on them. Their family will never allow any modern intervention to solve the problem. It's an ego issue for them. I can see that you both love each other, but that's not going to solve the issue. You have to take an initiative to save your marriage. You only can do that and I am here to help you. I told you many stories from mythology about Kunti, Satyavati. It's permitted even in our puranas. Think with a cool head. All is fair in love and war". She patted Swathi affectionately on her back and rolled her oiled tresses into a neat bun. She left her to her thoughts and entered the kitchen to supervise the breakfast arrangements.

Karan followed Rajanna to the small clearing behind the mango plantation of Nagaratnamma. Swathi was waiting there for him, seated on mango clump. Rajanna left without a word or a backward glance. Karan was surprised to get a letter from Swathi after so many years asking him to come and meet her at the mango grove. They both looked at each other, remembering olden days when they were never able to meet or see each other at such a secluded area. "How are you Swathi"? Finally, Karan found his voice. The cool breeze swaying the paddy fields, the moon slowly travelling high in the horizon and the fluffy white clouds floating in the dark sky created a magical and serene atmosphere for the two old friends.

"I am good. How is your wife and family?" enquired Swathi. "We are good and I am lucky that my wife loves me and spoils me with too much affection. She is at her mother's place for her second delivery" said Karan smiling proudly. Swathi clutched his hand and said "Karan, I know it's wrong to ask you but please save my marriage. I have no other choice but to beg you shamelessly. Promise me you will help without anybody's knowledge" sobbed Swathi. Karan was thoroughly confused and said "please Swathi. Don't cry, will definitely help you, if it's possible and within my means". Later, he heard her request and was stunned. Though unwilling initially, he decided to help her just to save her life and marriage, as he very well know, the plight of a barren woman in our society. Their union was pure in its purpose and remained buried between the trio.

'Shanthi Bhavan' was decorated beautifully with floral garlands and gates were wide open to receive the guests arriving in flashy cars and bikes. Men in their silk kurta pyjamas and women resplendent in their colourful Kanjeevarams and Gadwals, wearing gold and diamond jewellery, entered the hall, to be warmly greeted by the eldest son and daughter-in-law of Gupta family. Chairs were laid for people to sit and servants were busy serving cool drinks and snacks to the invited guests. On the Dias, sat the proud parents Rajesh and Swathi with a child on her lap. The family Purohit chanted slokas invoking Gods to bless the child. The havan was completed with all stipulated rituals and finally the naming ceremony started. All eyes, actually ears, strained to listen to the name and Rajesh loudly announced the name 'Gopal'.

The hall reverberated with happy clapping by all the guests. Nagaratnamma and Swathi stole glances at each other and thought 'maternity is a fact, but paternity is a belief. "Let there be peace and tranquility in the house and my Swathi stay happy and blessed with her family', prayed Nagaratnam to the Almighty.

Rajesh stood up with Gopal in his hands and Swathi next to him to take blessings.

All the guests showered petals on Gopal and his proud father.

39

BOAT

Amma, amma, shouted Lakshmi, happily, running towards the group of villagers coming towards the river. Rajyam came running from the crowd and hugged Lakshmi to her bossom. "Talli, are you okay? All good? I was so worried when I heard that the boat you were coming from the city capsized. We all came running to check. Thank God, you are fine! Devudi daya (God's grace)", she prostrated on the ground, thanking God for saving her only child from death. The villagers were also happy to find her safe. Lakshmi was soaked to the bone and shivering uncontrollably. So, all of them immediately moved towards Rajyam's house, though all were curious to know how she survived.

On reaching home, Rajyam immediately arranged for dry clothes and hot water for bath. By the time Lakshmi had her bath, Rajyam made hot coffee and pakodas for everyone to celebrate her daughter's safe return. While having coffee, the village elders asked Lakshmi as to "how she managed to reach the shore in the pitch dark night" as the boat capsized in the middle of the river? They also knew that many lost their lives in that tragedy and they were expecting the same fate for Lakshmi too, to be frank. They were planning to start a rescue mission, in fact, looking for her body as she doesn't know swimming and was also scared of water. She rarely took the boat and always preferred to take a bus, though it was roundabout and a long journey to the city compared to the water way.

Lakshmi looked intently at them and said "you won't believe, if I say, I was saved by Yerranna."

There was an audible gasp from the crowd in the room. Yemite? Pichekinnda?(What? Have you gone mad?), asked Rajyam angrily!

How can a dead man save you? Have you lost your mind due to the accident? Did you hurt your head or something" she yelled at her daughter.

People stared at them in shock. There were loud murmurs in the room. All started talking animatedly, till Sitappa, the president of the village shouted to maintain silence.

Sitappa looked at Lakshmi and asked her "what do you mean? Yerranna, who died a decade ago saved you? You mean someone looking alike? isn't it ?" "No, it was Yerranna and he even sent his regards to all of you, the village elders" she added softly! There was a hushed silence in the room. A palpable tension in the air. People were scared, shell shocked and were waiting with bated breath.

Lakshmi glanced at all of them and stated "yes, the same Yerranna, who was beaten to death by all of you for a crime not committed by him. He wanted to reaffirm his innocence through me even though you all know the truth". She vividly remembered that day when Yerranna's family was pushed out of the village while Yerranna was beaten by all men of the village. Her mother closed all doors and windows and they stayed like that the whole night. Next day, the police arrived and did some enquiry as it created an uproar in the nearby villages too. An untouchable and daily labourer was killed and his remains were burnt. But as there was no complaint or evidence of crime, it went unreported.

Sitappa sat like a statue with his eyes shut. He could see the images of his daughter and Yerranna sitting under a tree chatting animatedly and laughing. When they were confronted by him, Yerranna said he was just helping her with some colloquial terms and he was called by herself. But Sitappa's daughter kept mum and quickly ran to the house. A livid Sitappa called his workers to beat and throw Yerranna and his family out of the village. But the matter went out of hand as rumours spread in the nearby villages about the incident and more and more upper caste people gathered. An untouchable entering a higher caste house! Unpardonable! People took whatever they could lay their hands on and finally, Yerranna was killed and his family was attacked and thrown out of the village. All the while, Sitappa's daughter kept quiet and played the victim card. But even Sitappa and villagers know that without her encouragement and help, an untouchable could never ever enter the village head's house to sit in the garden. But Yerranna had to pay a price for their false prestige.

And now Yerranna returned to haunt him.

Sitappa rose and quietly left the house. The villagers too followed him out and all were shivering with fear and trepidation.

Rajyam was shocked and sat in a corner without even blinking, breathing heavy.

Lakshmi went and sat next to her and took her arms in her hands and rubbed them gently.

"Don't worry amma. Yerranna was an enlightened soul. He doesn't carry hatred or enmity towards anybody. He even told me that it was you who alerted Sitappa about their meeting as you were jealous of them being a widow. He was only upset about Sitappa's daughter who actually wanted him and almost forced him to meet her always. But when caught, she just left him to his fate and acted innocent. That pained him more, he said. He saved me by pushing me to the shore and when I wanted him to come and meet you, he told me his story and just disappeared into thin air. Even now, I don't know whether it was Yerranna himself or his soul. This boat journey is a journey, I will remember forever, for eternity!!".

Both Rajyam and Lakshmi sat silently praying for peace to Yerranna and the village.

40

SANTA'S MAGIC

Amulya sat on the bench after completing her regular rounds of walk around the lotus pond in the park to rest her tiring feet. Sipping cool water from her flask, she was enjoying laughter and shouts of the small kids playing around in the grass. A young, smartly dressed lady with her young kid joined her on the bench. Amulya gave a friendly smile to the lady as they both sat on the bench. The month being November, the air was crisp and the boy shivered slightly and moved closer to his mother. Noticing that Amulya laughingly said to the boy "may be, you should ask Santa for a nice, fluffy sweater as Christmas gift!", the boy looked at Amulya and sneered "Huh! There is no Santa, stupid. It's just a lie parents tell their kids. My dad already told me, what he is going to get me as a gift! You are so old and still believe it's Santa who gives gifts on Christmas! ".

Amulya was stunned at the small boy's rudeness, while his mother smiled snugly at her and said "we tell him everything truthfully! We don't want him to believe in these lies of Santa's magic or fantasy tales. We teach him to be practical and know the truth behind all these stupid customs and practices". So saying, she caught the hand of the boy and moved away.

Amulya also got up as it was getting dark and started walking towards her house on the main road. But her head was in a turmoil. "Was it necessary to be so frank with kids all the time? Can't we allow them to believe in some magical and fantasy stories as small kids to kindle creative thoughts and ignite their imagination? As a kid, she believed in magic as chocolates suddenly appeared in her father's hand or a dress magically appeared in her cupboard, left there by Santa. It didn't cause any harm to her in the long run. On the contrary, it helped her in creating many magical stories and fantasies to tell her kids and students and gain popularity! Then, she suddenly remembered the letter her daughter wrote to Santa aeons ago and chuckled, turning her head in amusement. The memory of that incident was still fresh in her memory.

Ananya was five years old when Hari got an overseas appointment. Till that time, they were in Ahmedabad and lived in an apartment. Amulya celebrated Dussehra by arranging dolls as per South Indian tradition, Diwali by distributing sweets and with fire crackers and all other festivals and rituals with lots of enthusiasm. For Christmas, she kept a Christmas tree and Ananya loved decorating it with bells, fairies, reindeers and a big bright star on top. Apart from gifts kept at the tree,

Amulya, also used to drop small gifts in Santa's long boots bought from a shop. She used to hang those shoes in some corner and it was fun and adventure for tiny Ananya to find them. She could never forget the excitement on Ananya's face and the sparkle in her eyes when she opened those gifts. Though simple gifts, the thought that Santa got them for her, for being a good girl added magic to them.

Then came this news of them moving to another country and Ananya was very excited for her first flight experience. But when she boasted about this to her friends, Raju asked her that "how will Santa know your new address? In that case, you will not receive any gifts this year". This came as a shock to Ananya and the moment she reached home, she started crying. After knowing her problem, Ananya's grandfather gave her an idea. He told her to write a letter to Santa giving her new address. This brightened Ananya who immediately, with the help of her grandfather, drafted a lovely letter to Santa with her new address and gave it to Amulya for posting.

This was 25 years ago and Amulya still preserved that letter written by her little innocent daughter to Santa. Ananya is now working as a software engineer in a MNC in amchi Mumbai. Her belief in Santa's magic is still very much alive. She wears Santa costume to distribute gifts to kids at selected orphanages to spread happiness and cheer to them.

Fantasy and magic should never go out of our lives. They make our mundane life sparkle a little, thought Amulya and her step was lightened as if by magic and the very thought made her smile as she walked towards her house singing...

"Jingle bells, Jingle bells, jingle all the way......"

41

TEACHER'S PET

May I come in Ma'am? The voice from the door way stopped Archana in mid-sentence. She turned and saw Rahul standing at the door of the classroom.

"Come in Rahul, you are late and have missed one problem. Take it from your friends and in case of any problem, you can see me in the staffroom", said Archana, to the chagrin of her students. Archana continued her accounts class for another 40 minutes and left.

"What's the matter dude?" sneered Ramesh, "Archana ma'am is so sweet with you? Teacher's pet, aren't you? If we are late by a few minutes, she lectures us for an hour. Never allows late submissions of our assignments. But she always supports you. What's the secret?? "A few others joined the chorus and started bullying Rahul who was almost in tears, trying to defend himself and his ma'am's reputation. It was an uneven match between his whole class and Rahul.

Suddenly, "stop that", a voice thundered and everybody turned to see the Principal and Archana standing inside the class room. The Principal said "all of you back to your seats". Once normalcy resumed, he asked the class "you are all questioning why Archana is always favouring Rahul, right ? Not just questioning, you are all trying to find fault in their relationship. Shame on all of you! How many of you really know about Rahul? He lost his father three years ago. Though a bright student, he couldn't manage the college fees and decided to drop out. Archana ma'am came to his rescue and arranged for crowdfunding and managed his admission into our college. Rahul, on his part, was doing two part time jobs, one in the morning and one after the college. He is the sole earning member of his family consisting of his mother and younger sister. He is juggling his work and college and that's the only reason Archana ma'am tries to be little supportive and encouraging. You all are coming from a privileged background with parents taking care of all your needs. Whereas, Rahul is one who has risen to the occasion to lead a life of struggle, but never complained or cried inspite of all his difficulties. So, I hope you all got your answer ".

There was pindrop silence in the class. The Whole class sat with their heads bowed.

Slowly, Ramesh stood up and offered his apologies to both Archana and Rahul.

He even promised on behalf of the class that they will become better persons, worthy of being Rahul's friends.

42

PUPPET

Rasi was busy playing with her dolls in the verandah of their small two bedroom house. Ratna, her toddler sister came crawling from inside and quietly picked one doll from the floor. Her gleeful gurgle alerted Rasi who was busy changing clothes for one of her dolls. She immediately tried to snatch the doll from her sister and naturally, Ratna protested with a loud howl. An alarmed Rasi tried to shut her mouth with her tiny palms and at the same moment, Manjula came running from the kitchen. She took the doll from Ratna's hand and said "Rasi, be careful. Next time when your sister takes a doll, let her also play or you just call me. Don't shut her mouth or push her. You should share toys with her, okay? Enough play for now. Come in for lunch. You can play again in the evening after your afternoon siesta". She smilingly carried Ratna and turned to go inside, but was ambushed by a very angry Lakshmi!

"Yes, now Rasi can play only when you, the maharani allows her to play. You and your daughter decide whether she can play or not. She can't even have a doll of her choice. What's the use abusing you? My fate is that I lost my young daughter and am still living to see my grandchild being abused by the stepmother".

Eyes blazing with hatred, face red with anger, Lakshmi was looking like Kali,

ready to pounce on her enemy!!

Manjula meekly replied "you are mistaken amma. It's lunch time for kids, so I stopped them to feed them. I am just advising Rasi to share and play with her sibling and not to do any physical harm, as she is also young. That's all. Nothing serious". But Lakshmi just went on with her tirade and left only after hurling a few more abuses at Manjula.

Manjula went on quietly with her work. After feeding the children and putting them to bed for their afternoon nap, she sat in her room doing the needle work. At 1.30 PM, she heard the sound of Naresh's bike and she kept her materials down and went to greet him. After wash, he came to the dining table and sat down for lunch. He kept on chatting about his office and colleagues non-stop, but then suddenly, he noticed Manjula's silence and her sad face. He stopped his monologue and gently touched her face and asked "what's the matter? You look so glum. Something bothering you? Tell me, what happened.

"Why Lakshmi Amma always treats me like an enemy? We were colleagues in the office before our marriage and I married you knowing all about you. It was my choice to marry you and not due any obligation or coercion. I loved Rasi as my own child from day one of our marriage. Even she loves me and is happy with me. Nothing changed even after I had Ratna. I am taking care of both as my own. Never showed any difference between them. I am just being a mom and trying to teach them to share and care. I was only cautioning Rasi to be careful with Ratna, but amma took it otherwise and abused me so much. I love her and respect her but it hurts me that she still thinks I am an evil stepmother! Why everybody thinks that a stepmother can never be normal and loving?" Manjula poured out her sorrow and frustration.

Naresh smiled and said, "stepmothers were stereotyped as monsters and killers, right from our Puranas to the kindergarten tales. Stories of Garuda, Ayyappa to Snowhite and Hansel and Gretel, all talk about evil stepmothers. Society as it is, believes in it. So, I don't blame amma for her mistrust in you. She and many others were conditioned into thinking like that. It takes love of many Manjulas to prove them wrong and shatter their misconception. They are all puppets in the hands of the society and it's old norms. It takes time, love and patience on our part to prove them wrong. Amma lost her young daughter to complications during delivery and was completely shattered. Then, I remarried you and her sorrow turned into anger and hatred. We have to give her some more time to accept you and understand your feelings and affection. Till that time, we are puppets in amma's hands and have to grin and bear her hatred and abuse".

Manjula heard all this with utmost concentration and vowed to herself that she will win the love and affection of amma with her patience and love. She is not going to allow the age-old misconception and mistrust to win against her. With that fresh thought, she happily sipped the kheer she made on Rasi's request!!

43

IT'S MY LIFE

Hema just stepped out of her 2 bedroom apartment and was locking the main door when she heard her neighbours whispering. She turned around to see both her neighbours from the adjacent flats staring at her sniggering. Rama, her immediate neighbour asked, "Are you going out like that!!" and her expression was, as if Hema was going out stark naked! Hema looked at herself and said "yes, I am going to meet my daughter for lunch at Marriott. So, I thought I will dress up like her in Jeans.

Actually, these Jeans were a gift from her for my birthday a few years ago. But as you know, jeans are forever and I hardly wear them. And today, I teamed them with my new top. Hope it's looking fine', she replied with a smile and started climbing down the stairs without waiting for an answer. Her neighbours, both in their seventies disapproved her independence and her way of embracing and enjoying life in her situation and she was well aware of it.

She heard Rama's voice floating down the stairs loud and clear. 'Look at her. Sixty plus oldie and that too a widow, wearing Jeans and going out shamelessly. Her poor husband died recently, isn't it? Just because her name is Hema, she acts as if she is that famous film star Hemamalini !! Chee, chee, shameless. If the mother is like this, think about the daughter ! Hey Muruga!'. The ranting continued and Hema heard every single word. She quietly continued her walk and got into the Uber that was waiting.

At the Marriott, Hema was directed to the reserved table and was greeted by Rashmi, her daughter and Anil, her son-in-law. After the usual chitchat, they ordered food and drinks. While sipping their soup, Rashmi asked 'what's the matter? I can sense that something was wrong from the time you came in. Is everything okay, ma??' Hema smiled and said, 'nothing I can't fix' and changed the topic. Next two hours, the trio shared gossip from Rashmi's Microsoft office and Anil's law firm. Hema regaled them with some anecdotes and family memories. After the sumptuous lunch, they went to watch a standup comedy by Amit Tandon. After spending a fun filled afternoon with them, Hema returned home and was greeted by a sarcastic 'looks like you had fun' by her neighbours.

Hema just waved and entered her home, muttering to self, 'what's wrong with you people'. She took a hot shower, wore her comfy pyjamas and made a nice smoothie and then snuggled into her favourite overstuffed sofa. She pinged her childhood friend Saroja to share her distress.

'Why can't they appreciate the fact that, after losing my husband so suddenly, I managed to pick up my life and am living independently. Never troubled them or depended on them. Luckily, I receive Rajiv's family pension which is more than sufficient. I am healthy, active and just trying to be happy and live with dignity'.

'That's the problem', declared Saroja, after patiently listening to Hema's trouble with her neighbours. "whatever said and done, people, especially those traditional types, can't accept the fact that you, a widow, is living a normal and happy life.

You were supposed to stay indoors, crying or at least grieving. Not to show interest in life and be normal within a year of your hubby's death. They never had the freedom or courage to live according to their will. On top of that, you still look young and beautiful for your age. So, I don't blame them", guffawed Saroja and continued "Anyway, forget those jealous cry babies and tell me how the show was.". The two friends chatted for some more time and later, Hema, with a lighter heart, went to bed.

In the morning, while sipping her coffee and browsing the newspaper, Hema came across an advertisement. It was like a signal from the universe! She immediately called Saroja, whose son was a professional photographer and noted his number. After a short discussion on phone with Rakesh, she got ready and went to his studio in T.Nagar. Rakesh came out and greeted her, 'Aunty, so nice to see you. You are looking fabulous as usual. Please come in. I am so excited to make a portfolio for you'. And the next few days, Hema got busy shooting her portfolio with Rakesh and his assistants. The whole team praised her for the confidence and her ease in front of the camera. Finally done, looking at her printed portfolio, Hema said, 'whether I get a role or not, but this was an amazing experience for me. Thank you all for the help and motivation. I really had such a good time'. She then left the studio and moved on to her next mission.

Hema reached the office of 'Ideas Advertising' for her appointment with the directors. After a few days of rehearsals and shooting, she got selected for a small role in one commercial for a coffee brand. Hema celebrated her joy by inviting Rakesh and his team for a coffee, but kept it as a secret from others.

Finally, the shooting was done, approved and slated for release on television, on all major channels. She invited Rashmi, Anil, Saroja and Rakesh for dinner on the D-day and casually kept her TV on and asked them to watch the commercials at 7.25p.m.

And bang on, Hema appeared in a blue sleeveless blouse and chiffon saree, with her short salt and pepper hair and twinkling eyes, enjoying her coffee on a swing for a few seconds, before the camera moved on to the others in the commercial.

Immediately, everyone jumped up clapping and hugging and congratulating Hema.

Champagne was opened and the meal prepared by Hema was consumed amidst lot of fun and everyone teasing Hema for autographs and selfies. Rashmi was so happy and proud of her mother that she messaged all her friends to watch the ad. Others followed her suit and did the same. That night, Hema went to bed very happy and proud of herself.

'I am very happy and proud to receive this prestigious 'Best Ma' award for my role in 'Modern Indian Ma' Hindi serial on Zee TV. I thank my family, friends and my neighbours for this award. I was a simple housewife, happy looking after my family. That was my whole world. I was into drama and music in my school and early college days and won many prizes too. But later, I got busy with academics, then my marriage and motherhood and my passion was put on a back burner. Many years later, I again enjoyed dabbling in drama, just as a hobby, when my husband was posted abroad. I acted in and directed a few plays for various cultural programs there. But never seriously pursued it. With the sudden demise of my husband, there was a vacuum in my life and I tried to fill it by doing something I always loved, teaching music. I was happy with my music, my students and spending my time with family and friends. But I was constantly criticised by many for my way of dressing, my outings and basically living life on my own terms. I am sixty plus, so I have to follow certain rules and regulations, of which I was reminded constantly and not so politely!

I know, I am not answerable to anyone. But still, just to prove a point, I went ahead and did a few commercials. And when I was approached for this role of modern ma, it was like a bolt from the blue. And I am so glad that my role was appreciated by all of you. Because this story is about me, in the real sense. It represents my thoughts, ideas and what I believe in.

I am totally humbled and honoured by your love and appreciation. But please extend the same love and understanding to the people around you. Whatever may be the the age and status, everybody around us here have their personal problems and are fighting their own battles. Don't make it difficult by your constant criticism.

If you can help, please do. Otherwise, just leave them alone. Live and let live.

Thank you, one and all. Hema ended her thank you speech and the hall reverberated with a thunderous applause. Her friends in the front row joined the applause, while Rashmi and Anil whistled loud.

And her neighbour's reaction, who were watching all this on TV, that's for another story...!

44

WINKING AT LIFE

The house was decorated tastefully with floral garlands and lights. Soft music was playing in the background. The interiors were decorated with diyas and marigolds.

Guests were all seated around the tables, chatting and enjoying their drinks and appetisers. A gigantic table was set up with a big wedding cake. The streamers and a banner announcing, 'Diamond wedding anniversary of Sagar and Rajani'

Swati was busy moving from table to table, meeting and greeting the guests.

Suddenly a gong was sounded and an announcement was made by Shankar, 'get ready to welcome the bride and the groom !!'. Everyone started clapping and cheering. Slowly entered Sagar, looking dashing in a dark blue full suit and a radiant Rajani, in a matching peacock blue Kanjeevaram saree, holding hands of their grand children Chitra and Shyam. After meeting the guests and a few speeches and general bantering, the cake was cut and champagne was opened. With music, dance, mouthwatering delicacies and desserts, the guests had a gala time. Swathi and Shankar planned everything meticulously for this special celebration. Swathi wanted this day to be a memorable day for her loving parents.

Finally, the party was over and the family sat down with tired, but with beamingfaces. Sagar said, "that was a wonderful party!! Enjoyed so much meeting all our friends. A big thanks to both of you for organising it so well. God bless you".

An emotional Rajani just hugged Swathi, Shankar and the kids.

After good nights, everybody moved to their respective rooms.

After changing into their night dresses, both Rajani and Sagar went and stood in the balcony, looking at the full moon.

With a chuckle, he said, "we completed 60 years together and do you remember, you had turned down my proposal initially". 'Yes,I did', said Rajani with a wink .

And both remained silent, holding hands and reliving the past.

............................" ....

The canteen of Gautam college of Management was full and in utter chaos as usual, with students milling in and out, chairs being dragged across to form groups, people weaving in between the tables with trays laden with food and drinks. Sagar was sitting alone, in a corner with eyes glued to his book, while sipping his hot cappuccino.

He heard a sweet voice asking, 'may I?' and lifted his eyes from the book to see an attractive girl, with a tray in her hand, pointing to the empty chair in front of him.

Certainly.....he replied and she pulled the chair and sat down with a smile and winked. It was so unexpected, Sagar almost choked on his coffee. 'I am extremely sorry', she muttered and her face went crimson. Sagar tried to cover the embarrassment by introducing himself, 'I am, Sagar, final year MBA' to which she replied 'Rajani, new admission' in a yankee accent and looking at the confusion on his face, added, just moved in from Connecticut'. 'What? ! I know people going to US to study but this is news', exclaimed Sagar. She winked again and before Sagar could say anything, Rajani said 'I think it's my lack of sleep due to the jet lag, my eyes are doing overtime, sorry'. Both had a hearty laugh and chatted for some time and before departing, exchanged their mobile numbers. From that day, their friendship grew and moved from canteen to restaurants and parks to movies. During their meetings, Sagar noticed Rajani's winks and some clumsy movements, but never mentioned it to avoid any friction in their friendship. Finally, Sagar graduated with flying colours and got into a multinational company, through a campus interview. But luckily, he was posted in Hyderabad only. They continued their meetings almost everyday without fail, except when Rajani flew to Connecticut for a three week vacation after completing her exams. After her return, on the day of second anniversary of their friendship, Sagar gathered his courage and proposed to Rajani in the boat, moving on the Hussain Sagar lake. He went down on his knees with a twinkling diamond ring in his hand ....Rajani winked, then blinked and started crying to Sagar's consternation. 'What happened? Did I say anything wrong? I thought you also have the same feelings. I am sorry, but Rajani stopped and hugged him tightly saying 'I love you so much but I can't marry you. I am the unlucky one'! and started sobbing again. With much cajoling and coaxing, Rajani said 'I had brain tumour and was operated. That was the reason I went to Connecticut for my medical review. According to Doctors, I may live upto 5 years. I am still on medication and that's what caused my winking and clumsy movements sometimes. I know you had noticed but never questioned or showed any difference. The reason for moving from my home and staying here with grandparents is for that only. All my friends and family show sympathy and treat me with utmost care. I was fed up of being treated like a glass doll about to break. I moved here to lead a normal life and be independent as much as possible. Fate intervened and I met and fell head over heels in love with you but I can't ruin your life with my health problems and uncertain future. You deserve a partner who will be with you throughout your life to love and support you, for which, Sagar replied, 'is there any guarantee for my life or future? Anything can happen anytime to anybody. Life is unpredictable for all of us. Who are these doctors to decide your life span? Remember Stephen Hawkins?? He was given two years to live. And he lived a full life, married twice, created history with his scientific theories. Why, so far? Our Amitabh came out of the jaws of death after his accident and look at him. Energetic and active even now. Let's not fear the unknown future and spoil the present. Let's celebrate each day as it comes and enjoy.

Finally, Sagar managed to convince her and triumphantly put his ring on her finger and kissed her for the first time. The boatman winked and showed a thumbs up to Sagar.

The marriage was a simple affair with close family and friends. Rajani's family was over the moon at this unexpected twist in their daughter's life and made all arrangements for the couple's new wedded life. Sagar's parents, though initially worried, accepted their son's decision and welcomed Rajani into their fold with much love and affection.

Rajani enjoyed every moment of her life. She took up yoga and meditation which calmed her mind and removed the anxiety and fear. She started a small business venture and it was flourishing. She was counting her blessings and thanking her God, when another wonderful thing happened. She conceived and without any complications, gave birth to a beautiful child. They named her Swathi. Even her doctors were baffled, when they found that the scan showed no tumour. And they attributed it to her positivity and active life full of love and laughter.

This gave idea to Rajani that she should help people like her who were survivors of some serious diseases like tumours and cancer to lead a normal life without any dread or stigma. With the help of Sagar and few like minded friends, Rajani started a support group to reach out and help all those survivors. She conducted seminars, did talk shows, sharing her life's journey, spreading the message of positivity and encouraging them to become active and lead normal lives. She touched so many lives who became like an extended family. Many of whom attended the function too,

to show their appreciation.

Rajani moved closer and hugged Sagar 'Thank you for this wonderful journey!!

WISH

Lakshmi came out of her reverie with her mother's loud voice saying,

"hey, scrub well and fast! Always day dreaming". She looked sheepishly at her mom Mangi and started scrubbing the vessels vigorously. "We still need to clean the house and arrange all the chairs. The guests may start arriving any moment from now", chided Mangi.

"Today, Kalyani akka is looking so beautiful in her new silk saree. I wish I too can wear one just like that", said Lakshmi. Her mother gave one hard slap on her back and said "just now what did tell you? Do you know how much is that saree? It costs almost one year of my salary. So, stop this nonsense and get going. From the last one month, this is what you are doing. Ogling the saree from the day she purchased it. I made a mistake of sending you with Kalyani papa, to help her in her shopping. You both are of same age and she treats you well. But Lakshmi, our status and their status are different. We just work for them, but luckily for us, they are nice people and treat us like family. For the past 15 years, we are staying in the outhouse and God only knows how well they treated us, giving shelter and respect. But you know, we should never ever cross the limits. Now come, let's finish the work before amma starts shouting" so "saying, Mangi took the cleaned vessels, stalked them nicely in a tub and hurried to the kitchen. Lakshmi followed her quietly and started cleaning the hall with the broom.

Lakshmi finished cleaning and started arranging the room. A huge van stopped at the gate and about a dozen girls attired in silk sarees similar to Kalyani's, but in a different colour, jumped out of it. All laughing and shouting, entered the house and surrounded Kalyani. College mates of akka, sighed Lakshmi and continued with her work. Suddenly, Kalyani beckoned her. She had a beautiful silk saree in her hands, which was similar to what her friends were wearing. She said "all my friends are going to be my bridesmaids and dancing to the popular Telugu movie songs during my Sangeet. You are a wonderful dancer and know all the steps. So now, go get ready in this saree and join my friends.

Lakshmi was speechless. What ?? Her wish had come true, in this beautiful way!!!!

She stood with her mouth open, gazing into Kalyani's face. Kalyani laughingly slapped her and said "hey you thought I will just marry and go away without thinking about my childhood friend? I know you loved my saree but I just wanted to surprise you. Now go, go. Get ready and come'.

Lakshmi impulsively hugged her and with tears flowing from her eyes, ran to show her mother, her WISH shining in her hands.

46

VENOM

Gita and Rita were walking down the road in silence, both engrossed in their own thoughts. Actually, Rita was fuming inside, "how dare this Gita ki bacchi complain to Dad about me? I will bunk classes, go out of college, so what? Just because no one looks at her ugly dark face, carrying stories to Dad! Eh! And on top of it, she says it's her duty as my elder sister to protect me from bad influences! My foot! Born two minutes before me doesn't give her that right! This conversation was going on in her mind.

While Gita was thinking, "thank God, today I managed to talk to Dad about that rascal Vinod, who, after going around with many girls, is now after Rita. And this stupid girl has fallen for him and is painting the town red, bunking classes and making excuses for coming late, saying extra classes. Hope she will now stop all this nonsense".

They walked into their respective classrooms and got busy with the lessons and other activities.

Rita was fair, tall and very beautiful. She, with her large eyes, dark curly hair and a oval face, was exactly opposite to Gita. Though she beat Rita in academics, music and cultural activities, Gita lost in the beauty department. Tall, dark and with her nondescript features, it's difficult to accept her as a twin to Rita. Gita took after her father, while Rita is a replica of her mother.

Rajaram was a self-made millionaire. He came up in life with his talent and hard work and always encouraged his daughters to excel in all fields. He openly praised Gita for her achievements and told Rita to learn from her. Though he meant to encourage Rita, it did create a sort of rift between the twins. Unknowingly, Rajaram created a ripple and her brother-in-law Shyam turned it into a whirlpool.

Rajaram belonged to a middle class family but with hard work, he started a company and slowly raised in position. But he never forgot his roots and remained a simpleton. He married Sujatha, his classmate in a simple wedding and also accepted her wayward brother Shyam. He tried his best to settle Shyam into some job but he never stayed in any but just enjoyed his drinks and other addictions for which, his sister supplied money secretly. Though Sujata loved her brother and provided shelter and took care of him, Shyam was always jealous of her status as a millionaire's wife. He secretly made Rita a pawn in his hands. He sowed the seeds of jealousy in her from childhood by always pitying her about the way her father admonished her, while praising Gita. His constant narrative and small gifts turned her against both Rajaram and Gita. But one day, Sujatha overheard this and banished him from the house. But he secretly kept in touch with Rita and vowed to take revenge on the family.

Vinod and Rita sneaked out of college and as usual, went to the nearby park. Rita was still angry at Gita and was like a volcano, about to erupt. Suddenly, she stopped in tracks as a smiling Shyam came out of the bushes, with a gunnysack in his hand. "Mama(uncle), she shouted in joy and went to him. He patted her on her back and looked at Vinod and said "good selection". And Rita blushed and said "isn't it? And that vampire Gita told all kinds of stories about him and made Dad very angry. He sternly warned me against meeting Vinod. But who cares? Anyway, he always supported her, like you always said". Vinod looked nonchalantly at them. Shyam was fiddling with the gunnysack and suddenly heard an angry voice "what are you doing here? How dare you talk to Rita". Vinod and Rita turned swiftly towards the voice to see a very angry Gita staring at Shyam. In this confusion, Shyam dropped his sack and a whitehood peaked out and caught him on his ankle.

He screamed aloud and dropped to the ground. A slithering albino cobra came out of the sack and plunged it's fangs into his thigh and swiftly moved towards a frozen Vinod and punctured his foot and then vanished into the bushes. Gita was the first person to recover and ran shouting for help, while pulling Rita along.

Two days later, Vinod from the hospital bed, gave his confession to the police. In which he confessed that on the behest of Shyam, he approached Rita and made her fall in love with him using the tactics taught by Shyam. He was told by Shyam to bring her to the park that day but was not aware of Shyam's plan of killing her to take revenge on Rajaram. Police investigation revealed that Shyam befriended a guard at MCBT and smuggled a caged cobra. And ironically, he was killed by the same cobra and Vinod was saved by the anti-venom produced by the same MCBT. (Madras Crocodile Bank Trust) He was saved as most of the cobra's venom was used on Shyam and only a little entered his blood stream. Rita finally understood how she was made a puppet by her own jealousy and mistrust on her family. Finally the twins were now united in the true sense.

DOUBLE STANDARDS

"Come on, drink your medicine please", pleaded Payal, holding the small measuring cup in her hand. "Noooo, it's very bitter", said Mohan, rolling his eyes.

"Please, just gulp it and you can then have this Cadbury, Payal tried to cajole.

After a lot of begging and threatening, Payal finally succeeded and came out of the room triumphantly.

"How do you manage this drama everyday? It's getting too much", said Rajesh with disgust." Most of your time and energy are wasted on him", complained Rajesh.

"Today, he was refusing the medicine and not listening to the nurse. So, I went to give him food and medicine. Now, he will sleep like a baby. Come on, let's have some coffee. I need some petrol urgently", said Payal with a smile and went into the kitchen.

"Why don't we admit him in a nice old age home? They take care of him well, as they have trained people. We just have to pay a deposit. And we can visit him often. I know a few places and if you want, we can go and have a look", suggested Rajesh. Payal quietly continued with her work of making their coffee. Rajesh followed her and took his cup and sat opposite her at the dining table. He started talking excitedly about the wedding plans and the shopping, etc, etc.

After a few sips, Payal asked Rajesh "what about your parents? Are they going to stay with us after marriage?" "Yes, of course. I am their only son, so it's natural, you see. And you don't have to bother about locking the house, managing servants, etc. Mom will manage everything. You just have to go to office and take care of us. That's all" Rajesh winked and gave a broad smile.

"But I can't take care of my own father. Isn't it? Double standards! You were a regular at our house from our university days. Enjoying dishes prepared by my mom, playing chess with my dad. You knew him for long. How happy and independent he was. When you proposed to me, he was the happiest person. He met your parents and did all the necessary arrangements for our engagement. He even made elaborate plans for our wedding. But unfortunately ended up in a terrible car accident. Due to which, I not only lost my mother, but my father too, in a way. He lost his memory and became a child due to that shock. Now, I can't just leave him for your sake, forgetting all the pampering and love he showered on me and on us.

Sorry, you wasted one year waiting for me but this gave me an opportunity to see your true colours. You are happy to marry me, with my 5 digit salary and property but you don't care for a 70 year old who behaves like a seven year old. When he was well, he treated you like his son, but unfortunately, you never saw a father in him. You just want him to be sent away to a home. Abandon him just like that. It's okay for you, but not for me.

You don't have to bother looking for a home for him. He is in his home with his daughter. I was observing you for the past few months, the way you were getting irritated with my father. No more of it. You please go home and never come back here. We are done.

This coffee is your last drink in this house and with me. Goodbye", said Payal, with her head held high.

48

JUST ANOTHER DAY

Anuradha woke up with the first rays of the sun slanting through the window. She stirred and remained in the bed. muttering, just another day! Nothing to do, nothing to look forward to! No one even to ask, whether she had eaten or not. Her eyes swelled with tears and she sobbed silently into her pillow. Sighing, she wiped her wet cheeks and tried to sleep for some more time. Finally, bored of lying in the bed she got up and freshened up. Later, she made some tea, but sat looking vacantly at the walls, immersed in her thoughts. By the time she remembered to drink, the tea turned cold and she just went and dropped the cup in the sink mechanically. She had stopped making any effort to cook or eat after her husband Mohan's sudden death. She was yet to come out of that shock. Living alone in that house surrounded by his personal things and memories was like solitary confinement. Whenever she was hit by severe hunger pangs, she just reached out for some fruit or bread. She rarely cooked and hardly stepped out of the house. Just counting days for her death was her favourite sport now.

Their's was a love marriage against their parents' wishes as they belonged to different castes. They got married with the help of friends, but were disowned by their own families. They moved on with life and were happy in their own small world. They bought a small flat, arranged it tastefully and were ready and eagerly waiting for a new addition to their love nest. But God had other plans and Mohan contacted covid. He was immediately taken to the hospital but his lungs got affected and he lost his battle against death. The shock left the young Anuradha utterly shattered. Even Mohan's death didn't bring any change in the attitude of their respective parents. His parents blamed her for his death, while her parents kept their distance as they had her younger siblings yet to be married off. Left alone, Anuradha lost interest in her life and was just there like a shadow of her previous self. Their friends tried to reach out to her, but Anuradha went into a shell and refused to meet or talk to anyone. Her grief took over her completely!

Lost in her thoughts, Anuradha suddenly heard a faint wail of a child from her front yard. She came out of her trance and quickly ran in that direction. There, bundled up in a soft cotton saree, a chubby baby girl was crying at the top of her voice. Anuradha immediately picked her up and tried soothing her by rocking her and cooing softly. Guessing that the baby must be hungry, she hurried inside and tried feeding her some warm milk with a spoon. After few spoons of nourishment, the baby gurgled happily and snuggled to Anuradha's bosom and fell asleep. Though she was smitten by the baby, Anuradha called and informed the Police about the abandoned baby.

The police came and took a few pictures and identification marks of the baby to post in the newspapers. A doctor checked and found out the baby to be about ten month old, healthy and fit. On Anuradha's request, the police allowed her to take care of the baby till they found her parents or family.

Anuradha was now once again her usual happy self. She found a reason to live and a commitment to nurture another life. More than two years had passed, but police were unable to get any clue about the baby's parents. Except the cotton saree she was bundled in, there was nothing on the baby to help the police in their investigation and the case was closed. An overjoyed Anuradha adopted the baby and named her Mohana. She got busy with her online job and full time motherhood. No time to mope or cry now.

From just another day, Anuradha moved to another wonderful day!

49

VATSALYA

The garden was reverberating with children's laughter and shouts. Mingling into that,one could hear elderly voices having fiery debates on latest politics, movies and general chatter. This was 'VATSALYA' , a unique home for orphan kids and elderly. It was the brain child of Dr. Madhav, who started a Home with just one octogenarian who was abandoned at his Versova clinic. His patient Jayaram Naik was admitted for a stomach ailment. But after admitting him, his son went away without any trace. Even police failed to locate his whereabouts. Moved by the plight of Jayaram, Dr.Madhav shifted him to his outhouse and made arrangements for his stay. Slowly, the number of abandoned in various hospitals and streets brought to his notice kept increasing. So, with the help of a few likeminded friends, he started an old age shelter for the abandoned. It grew with the help of donations from friends and his clients. One of his clients was running an orphanage for young street children. When Madhav visited the orphanage to do a free medical check-up, an idea struck him. He always noticed that inspite of all the facilities and care, his elderly inmates still missed their families, mostly the grandchildren. That made them moody and irritable for which, there was no medicine. Few got into bouts of depression and anxiety, which was affecting their general health, while the kids here were missing the warmth of their families. Some turned in to rebels, while some sulked. They were deprived of the guidance and needed nurturing for healthy growth of mind and body. Why not bring them together to make it a complete home where young and old could mingle and fulfil each other's needs?

Dr. Madhav discussed his idea and got a thumbs up from all his stakeholders and 'VATSALYA' was born. The small idea of Dr. Madhav changed the scenario at the shelter completely. Now, the elderly were kept busy as volunteers at the primary school to teach and mentor the kids. Cooking, painting, carpentry, needle work and many skills were taught with love and care. Stories, reading and sports were included in the daily schedule.

Now, the elderly were very busy with no time to brood and kids were happy and blooming. Both the abandoned souls found solace in each other. The model of bridging this gap was much discussed and appreciated and brought many accolades to VATSALYA and it's team.

This unique shelter program was hailed and emulated by many states. Dr. Madhav was honoured by the Maharashtra Government for his exemplary service to the society. Replying to the honour Dr. Madhav said "I fervently hope there will be no need for such shelters in future. Hope families realise their responsibility and take care of their elderly well. And youngters understand and take responsibility for their action. Then every home will be a "Vatsalya".

50

DEFEAT

Sanjay slammed the door of his SUV in a foul mood and walked unsteadily into his mansion. Kamala came out hurriedly from inside to hold his hand and helped him to climb the steps. "Where is your ladla? Having a party to celebrate his 50% marks"? shouted Sanjay.

"No, he is in his room" replied Kamala. "All were talking about their kids marks, achievements in IIT and Medicine, while having drinks and I, like a fool, sat there with my mouth shut, thanks to our son" lamented Sanjay. Kamala didn't reply but, quietly arranged the plates for dinner, as she knew that one word from her and the night would erupt into fireworks. They had their dinner in an uneasy silence except for the clatter of spoons.

Sanjay went upstairs to his bedroom to rest but heard a song coming from his son Dhruv's room. He slowly walked towards it and looked in. Dhruv was sitting in a corner, playing his guitar and singing a soulful song in Telugu. The room was filled with soft light and the fragrance from the Night Queen blooms from the garden blew through the open window. Looking at his son sitting so serene in his room, Sanjay lost his cool. He slapped him hard on his cheek and shouted "Are you not ashamed of yourself? You got 50% in your graduation, that too in stupid, useless B.sc and are chilling here as if you have got a great award. I am paying for all your idiosyncrasies. I am so ashamed of you. First time in my life, I felt defeated. I planned my life to the T and executed well, but you, the unwanted and unplanned one spoiled everything.

Saying I am completely defeated", he went back to his room in long strides. Kamala, who followed him upstairs stood aghast and looked at Dhruv's stunned face.

Sanjay, came from a poor but a very loving family. His father was a farmer and his brother followed his footsteps. But Sanjay hated that poverty and luckily for him, he was intelligent and always got good marks in school. Both his father and brother slogged and helped Sanjay in achieving his goal. He studied engineering and got a gold medal and a merit scholarship for higher studies. He did well and ended up in a plum job with a fat salary. He married a girl of his choice after looking at her family background and wealth. He kept his family away from him as he was ashamed of their illiteracy and poverty. Kamala always hated his selfish ways but kept quite to maintain peace in the family. Sanjay wanted only two kids and both Rahul and Ratna were bright and beautiful. As a cardinal rule in South Indian families, Rahul did engineering and Ratna went for medicine. Now, Rahul was doing his post-graduation in IIM Ahmedabad, just like his dad and Ratna was in her final year of medicine in Chennai. When Kamala got pregnant for the third time, she has not realised till it was well advanced, as her cycle was pretty irregular of late and she was also on the pill. Sanjay was very unhappy but as it was dangerous for Kamala he had to bite the bullet.

Dhruv was a very happy and bright kid but for him, academics were not everything.

He loved to paint, play guitar and sing. He was also a voracious reader and can talk about anything or everything under the sun. He loved to meet people and learnt from them. He was very different from his siblings, who idolized their father. While Dhruv was sensitive and simple, just like his mother. So, clashes between Sanjay and Druv were pretty common, but today it reached it's ugly height.

Next morning, Dhruv came down with a small suitcase and his guitar and went straight to his parents. He said "what dad said was correct. I enjoyed a luxurious life but did nothing in return. I am a graduate now and should find my own feet in the world, just like dad did when he was young. I too should find my way on my own. So, I am leaving now, but don't worry amma. I will regularly update you about my life". So saying he took his belongings, and went away quietly leaving his stunned parents behind. Kamala knew that behind the soft Dhruv, there was a strong willed person. She prayed for her ladla and hoped for the best, as she knew that he headed for his paternal grandfather's house in the village with whom both Kamala and Dhruv were always in touch in-spite of Sanjay's refusal to have anything with them.

Dhruv reached his grandfather's village and basked in the love of his grandparents' and uncle's family. His uncle has one son, Ramesh. He slowly started going to the fields along with his uncle and Ramesh and learning the age old practices followed by them and also comparing them with the new technology available now. He came up with good suggestions combining both and started organic farming. And as water was scarce in that area he came up with alternatives like millets, which need less water and more in demand now in the cities as wonder food. Dhruv with his sweet simple ways, attracted everyone in the village and managed to establish a co-operative with most of the farmers as members. He, with the help of his friends in the city, started an online market chain for their produce, reducing transport and other overheads. The income of the villagers doubled in no time. He got other facilities too by approaching the higher authorities. The officials too very happy to see the village prosper well under his guidance and extended their full support. Dhruv started a youth club where youngsters could play carrom, basketball, cricket, etc. He also taught guitar and singing for recreation and got good educative books and newspapers from the city and started a small library and inculcated reading habit in the children. In four years time, Dhruv became the talk of the town for his innovative ideas and implementation. The whole village adored him and for children, he became a hero, their idol. Their village became a model village and other village heads too started consulting Dhruv.

Dhruv kept his promise to his mother and sent letters about his work and also took valuable advice from her. He met her during his visits to the city. She wholeheartedly supported him in his mission to transform the village and was very proud of his accomplishments.

Sanjay was having his bed coffee, when Kamala came in with the newspaper and a beaming face and showed him the headlines. The 'Young Achiever for the year 2019' for the state of Telangana goes to Dhruv Kumar from Sarangapur and a smiling face of Dhruv was looking at him. His grandfather and uncle were standing on either side of Dhruv with pride.

Tears made the picture blurry and Sanjay mumbled "today he truly defeated me. The son whom I regarded as useless and a loser, is adored and loved by thousands.

He taught me how to live life with simplicity and dignity and with the loved ones".

51

LATE

"Naannamma, don't worry. We are not your responsibility. In fact, you were supposed to be taken care of by dad. I will find some work and manage". Raju's words brought fresh tears to Lakshmamma's eyes. She pulled Roja closer and said "you are not my responsibility! You both are my lifelines. I always fought against odds in my life but had never given up on hope. I always stood firmly against all calamities and faced life squarely! I will continue that my dear. I fail to understand, how my own son was such a coward and gave up all in one moment! Let it go! You and your little sister Rani, just concentrate on your studies and enjoy life. Be strong and learn to face life in all it's vagaries. Don't give up like your parents. You are my hope and strength. I still have a lot of fire in me. Let me handle the situation and you just relax and take care of Hima. Poor little thing, she is so confused and bewildered. Just be with her. Let me finish cooking and let's have our dinner. Later, I will tell you stories. Okay"? She wiped her face with a new resolution and walked into the kitchen with her mind racing hard with ideas.

Lakshmamma was left with a five year old son and a dilapidated house attached to five acres of land when her husband died of snake bite while working in the farm.

Without any support from the family, she managed tending the farm with the help of workers. Later, she learnt the techniques of farming from the agriculture department bulletins on radio. She even started a poultry farm to supplement the income for her son Harish's higher studies. Harish was a meritorious student and bagged a seat alongwith a scholarship and reduced some of her burden. She still helped him when he wanted to go abroad for studies by selling her poultry. He promised to make up for the financial loss once he is settled, but later completely forgot about it in his race for dollars. He married his colleague Ratna and both worked hard and made a cosy nest for themselves. A visit by them after a gap of four or five years was what Lakshmamma was entitled in all those years. Even during that time, he stayed with his family in the city hotel as they couldn't tolerate the dirty village atmosphere. Though Lakshmamma felt disappointed with his attitude, she never expressed it. 'What an irony, the very village farm and poultry paved way for his future' she thought to herself. She enjoyed meeting her grandkids and they too developed a bond with her, during those short stays.

Suddenly, the news of double suicide of her son and daughter-in-law shattered her. She was told about their financial difficulties and the drastic step taken by them. Harish and Ratna both lost their jobs and in no time the money saved was gone. The car and their house were mortgaged. They were unable to find another job and felt humiliated to take help from their parents. Used to the lavish life and luxurious comforts, the stress and strain became unbearable to such an extent that both Harish and Ratna committed suicide by consuming poison. Luckily, they spared the kids and sent them to their friend's house with a letter addressed to Lakshmamma, apologising and requesting her to take care of the kids.

It was a hard blow to Lakshmamma and she was completely shattered. But Raju's words rekindled her spirit and she was ready to face the world again for the sake of her grandkids. She lost her son by not imbibing in him self-confidence, resilience and patience. She always shielded him from problems, taking all the burdens on herself. She realised her mistake now. Better late than never. She pledged that she will raise her grandkids like warriors, capable and confident to face the ups and downs of life without succumbing to it's pressure.

A mother never tires or retires when her kids are in need of help and support.

52

TOMORROW

Vaishnav was busy checking his mail on his laptop and his mobile chimed, showing the caller as amma. 'Oh, God, I forgot to call dad on his birthday. Now, she will take me to task and lecture me for an hour about children's irresponsibility and carelessness and blah blah blah! I am not in a mood for that', he mumbled to himself and left the phone unanswered and continued with his work. The mobile stopped after ringing for a long time and then it beeped signalling a message. Vaishnav ignored that too. I am not seeing or replying to her now. Let her cool down a bit. Will call her tomorrow and apologise to her and dad too. Meanwhile, I will check and order something for Dad as his birthday gift and one for mom to butter up, he chuckled.

Vaishnav, being the only son, was doted on by both his parents. He was born after ten years of their marriage, that too after a long medical treatment of his father and many a prayer and fasting by his mother. They fulfilled all his whims and fancies from his childhood, but he never misused his freedom or privilege. He grew up with self imposed discipline and studied well and behaved well. He was a good and all round student, well admired by all his teachers and liked by his friends and classmates. He completed his engineering from IIT Kanpur and post-graduation in management from IIM, Ahmedabad. Though he got many offers from abroad, he decided to start his own company along with two of his friends. Everything was going on well but now he got into the rat race of becoming a billionaire in a short period of time. To concentrate on business and avoid commuting time, he started living in a big house in the suburbs of Bangalore, which served as his office-cum-home. His parents understood his difficulties and supported his decision. He promised to visit them every weekend to spend some quality time with them. But now, he was so busy that his visits to home got postponed many times. Every time he promises, some urgent work crops up and he calls his mother to inform 'will come tomorrow, definitely'! Like that, many tomorrows came and went. Now, wishing them on birthdays and festivals also became a rarity. Everything was pushed to tomorrow, which never came! This time, as usual, he forgot his father's birthday, forget about going and meeting him at home, he didn't even call to wish him. He knew how angry his mother would be. Anyway, will visit them tomorrow, Vaishnav decided before going to bed.

Next morning, he got ready and got into his car. On the way, he thought of calling his mother but decided against it as he wanted to surprise his parents. He stopped at a famous bakery and picked up his father's favourite red velvet cake and a few baked paneer samosas. He also picked up a nice bouquet for his mother, hoping to cool her temper with those flowers. He happily drove his car into the compound of his parent's apartment building. He parked his car and took the elevator, while mentally preparing his apologies and waiting to see his father's child like glee on eying the cake box in his hands. He knocked on the door and waited with a grin on his face. The grin turned into frowns, as there was no response even after several knocks. He then thumped on the door and called out aloud. He then tried calling their phones, but got no response. In panic, he dropped all his gifts there and ran to the neighbors. He enquired with all their immediate neighbours and the watchman, but they had no clue. He called a few friends of his parents, but in vain. Vaishnav panicked and finally broke open the flat lock to check inside the apartment. The apartment was spick and span but there was no sign of the occupants. Everything was in it's place with no sign of any mishap. Finally, after trying everything, he went to the police to file a complaint but they advised him to wait for 24 hours after which they will initiate the proceedings. He came home tired, stressed, hungry and angry. He kicked himself for not answering his mom's phone even after repeated calls or atleast checking her messages. Then suddenly, he remembered the last message which he had not yet checked. He checked his mobile but it was deleted later by the sender. He scratched his head in despair. He couldn't eat or sleep and spent the whole night praying for the well-being of his parents.

Vaishnav took shower and was getting ready to go the police station when his door bell rang. The sudden shrill sound made him jump out of his skin. He recovered and ran to open the door in haste. He gave a shout of sheer joy seeing his parents standing there, alive, hale n hearty. Mom! dad! he shouted and rushed to hug them. He pulled them in and collapsed on a sofa. "Whew! What a relief, I am almost out of my mind with worry", he muttered. His mom looked at him and said, "why? Only parents were supposed to die a hundred deaths a day worrying about their kids? Not visiting, picking up phone and no repentance! That's the privilege, only for you kids?

Even parents can also act the same way. We too have a life", she countered.

Vaishnav hung his head and kept mum. He now realised how much he hurt his parents with his unruly behaviour. He made coffee and served it with some biscuits. He sat next to his mom and sheepishly asked "mom, atleast now please tell me, where did you go without informing anyone".

"We planned to go to a resort for your dad's birthday. I wanted to discuss with you and make plans for the trip. But you skipped coming home last week and then didn't even pick-up our calls. I was fed up and called the resort guy directly and he arranged the whole trip, including transport from our home. I called you to inform about it many a time, but you didn't pick-up the calls. Finally, I sent a message but you ignored that too. Later, around midnight, I got angry and deleted it. We wanted this 70th star birthday of your father just a family affair, so we had not informed any of our friends. We wanted it to be a relaxed one, without the usual party. Just a day to spend in gratitude to God and our parents for this beautiful journey of life. So, we went ahead without you and now returned, spending a whole day and night there" concluded his mom.

"I am really sorry, mom and dad. This time, I mean it. I now understood the pain and disappointment I caused you people by ignoring you and your calls. I now realised my folly. You will see a new Vaishnav from tomorrow!"

"Not again ! No tomorrow", shouted his parents in unison!